"If you expect me to pack up and leave without a fight, then you have another think coming."

"On the contrary, darlin'," he said, his smooth drawl at odds with the resentment she detected in his voice. "I fully expect you to stay."

Wariness pulsed through Josie with every heartbeat. Was he tricking her somehow? Letting her believe that he wasn't going to take away the only home she and Kellie had? "I...I don't understand."

"There's a stipulation to the deed," he said very carefully, as if he wanted her to understand what he was about to say. "A provision your father set and I agreed to before I won that last poker hand."

"What kind of stipulation?"

Seth O'Connor's smile was grim. "That we get married."

Janelle Denison has read romances ever since she was in high school. She never intended to become a writer, but her love of books and romance led to writing the kind of emotionally satisfying stories she's enjoyed from Harlequin over the years. While perfecting her craft, she worked as a construction secretary, but recently decided to quit her "day job" to write full-time.

Janelle lives in Southern California with her engineer husband, whose support and encouragement have enabled her to follow her dream of writing, and two young daughters, who keep life interesting and give her plenty of ideas for the young characters she includes in her books.

Janelle's greatest hope is that her romances leave her readers smiling and feeling as if they've made a couple of new friends. After all, nothing is more enjoyable and heartwarming than watching two opposites struggle against all odds, then fall in love despite those odds.

Bride Included
Janelle Denison

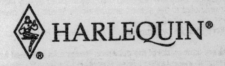

TORONTO • NEW YORK • LONDON
AMSTERDAM • PARIS • SYDNEY • HAMBURG
STOCKHOLM • ATHENS • TOKYO • MILAN • MADRID
PRAGUE • WARSAW • BUDAPEST • AUCKLAND

To all the wonderful friends I've made who have helped me along this incredible journey, from the struggles in the beginning, to sharing the joy of each sale. There are too many of you to name, but each one of you played a part in making this dream a reality.

And, as always, to Don, who makes every story special, just by believing in me.

RECYCLED PAPER · RECYCLED PAPER

ISBN 0-373-03565-9

BRIDE INCLUDED

First North American Publication 1999.

Copyright © 1999 by Janelle R. Denison.

This edition published by arrangement with Harlequin Books S.A.

® and TM are trademarks of the publisher. Trademarks indicated with ® are registered in the United States Patent and Trademark Office, the Canadian Trade Marks Office and in other countries.

Look us up on-line at: http://www.romance.net

Printed in U.S.A.

CHAPTER ONE

"MOM!" Josie McAllister's ten-year-old daughter, Kellie, burst into the kitchen, her wide green eyes filled with panic. "There's a big man on a horse riding across the pasture. He's headed toward the house and he looks mean!"

Josie frowned and washed her hands, sticky from the biscuits she'd just cut out for dinner. "Are you sure it's not one of the ranch hands?"

"I'm sure!" Kellie's chest heaved with panting breaths and her face was flushed, as if she'd bolted across the hundred yards separating the stables from the main ranch house. "I've never seen him before!"

Josie wiped her hands on a terry towel, a twinge of uncertainty rippling through her. It was Sunday, and even though her foreman, Mac, usually stopped by to check on the stock, the rest of the hands spent the day with their families. She'd heard Mac pull his old beat-up Ford out of the driveway over an hour ago, which meant she and Kellie were alone.

Normally, that wouldn't be cause for concern. She'd lived in this house her entire life, and not once had a stranger or drifter threatened her or her father. She trusted the men they'd hired and had been lucky in that respect.

Tears filled Kellie's eyes, and she tugged urgently on her mother's arm, gaining her attention again. Josie wanted to believe her daughter was just being overly dramatic, but Kellie had never been the theatrical type. She was shy and mild-mannered, and had certainly never been prone to hysterics before.

Tossing the hand towel onto the counter, she gave her

5

daughter a reassuring smile. "Come on, let's go see who it is."

Instead of opening the front door as she'd normally do to greet a visitor, she gave in to caution and pushed back the cream sheers covering the window in the entryway. She glanced out just as a man dismounted from a beautiful chestnut down by the stables and draped the horse's reins on the hitching post.

The man *was* big—at least six foot two, with wide shoulders that tapered into a trim waist, lean hips and a horseman's thighs. Even from this distance, she could see he was physically fit, and even though he hadn't turned around so she could see his face, she instinctively knew he wasn't one of her men. None of her ranch hands had a presence like this cowboy, a natural air about him that commanded respect and authority.

He turned and strode purposefully toward the main house. Still, she didn't recognize him, but then the brim of his black Stetson cast shadows over his features. He wore a blue-striped Western shirt and a dark pair of jeans cinched at the waist with a heavy belt buckle.

"Mom, who is he?" Kellie whispered from beside her, as if the man had the ability to hear them.

"I don't know…" The rest of her sentence caught in her throat as the man pushed his hat back on his head, finally offering her a glimpse of his face. Everything inside her went cold, like the biting chill that swept through the Montana mountains in the winter.

Seth O'Connor, the boy who'd tormented her throughout grade school, and in high school had scorched her with kisses she'd never forgotten, stolen her virginity and her heart, then had spurned her, nearly destroying her in the process. That had been eleven years ago, and even though they hadn't spoken to each other since that day that had irrevocably changed her life, she'd seen him around town. He never looked her way, never gave any indication that she existed for him or that she'd ever meant anything more to him than the revenge he'd extracted.

She closed her eyes to block the painful memories. They'd been neighbors all their lives, her father's property adjoining Seth's father's land. Nearly a thousand acres separated their homesteads, and given the feud that had kept both families in contention for over seven decades, the chasm could have been the width of two continents.

"Mom, are you okay?"

Kellie's worried voice reached her, pulling her back from the past. She blinked her eyes open and her stomach lurched when she saw that Seth was more than halfway across the yard. His face looked grim, his stride quickly eating up the distance.

He didn't look like he was here on the Golden M for a social call. Feeling threatened as never before, she darted into the living room, grabbed the key above the glass-enclosed cabinet displaying her grandfather's rifles and inserted it into the lock. One sure twist and the panel swung open. She grabbed the rifle on the rack in front of her, yanked out the drawer beneath for ammunition. In less than fifteen seconds, the rifle was loaded and she was heading back toward the front door.

"Mom!" Kellie cried fearfully.

"Go up to your room and stay there!" Josie ordered, and waited while her daughter obeyed and was safely on the second landing before she walked out onto the porch and lifted the rifle, bracing the butt firmly against her shoulder and taking aim at the man's heart. "Stop right there, O'Connor."

To his credit, he immediately halted, putting him ten feet away from the porch steps and too close for Josie's comfort. His jaw clenched. He didn't like her having the upper hand—she could see it in the narrowing of his eyes, the subtle tensing of his cowboy-honed body.

She never believed she would stand this close to him

again, never believed she'd threaten him with a rifle, either. But she wasn't taking any chances where Seth O'Connor was concerned.

Their gazes met, his diamond hard and just as blue as she remembered, like the rippling, crystalline water in the north end pasture's creek. Eyes she'd once thought of as kind. Eyes that had seduced her with the sweet promise of being desired and cherished.

It had all been a ruse.

Her finger tightened on the trigger. "Get off my property," she said succinctly.

He lifted his hands to his hips, his stance deceptively loose. "Why, Josie darlin', I think you're making a mistake there." He was all drawl and cowboy charm, but his smile held a hint of danger. "It's *my* property."

What in the world was he talking about? She looked closer, searching for signs that he'd become a drunk like his father had been. He looked totally lucid. "Your property ended miles ago. I suggest you haul your butt back to your horse and leave before I shoot you for trespassing."

"Tsk, tsk," he said with a cocky, challenging air that caused a flicker of apprehension to crawl up her spine. "That red hair of yours sure does match your temper."

Hating his mockery and furious at his gall, she lifted the barrel of her rifle a foot and a half and pulled the trigger, clearing the hat right off his head. He instinctively ducked, but seconds after the fact, then slowly straightened, his mouth gaping in shock. She experienced a moment of satisfaction to see that he'd paled beneath that nice tan of his.

His shock gave way to pure fury. It ignited in his gaze and seemed to coil within his body. With the hot July sun glinting off his dark brown hair, he looked like a dangerous outlaw. "Goddammit, woman," he exploded. "You could have killed me!"

"Could have, but I didn't want to kill you, just give you a final warning." She chambered in another round and slowly lowered the barrel of the rifle to the zipper of his jeans. She smiled oh so sweetly. ''Next time I won't be so gracious.''

His blistering curses filled the air. With a low, enraged growl, he charged up the stairs, calling her bluff. Her heart leaped in her throat, and the first frisson of alarm ripped through her. She might have held the gun, but she'd never truly harm him, despite her threats. She only wanted him to leave.

He gained the porch and stopped, a feral smile curving his mouth. Then he started toward her, slow and predator-like. For every step he took forward, she went back, until her spine slammed against the side of the house and there was nowhere left to go.

He jerked the rifle from her grasp and tossed it aside. It hit the wooden floor with a loud crash and skittered to the opposite side of the porch. Refusing to cower like some helpless female, she abruptly came at him, fists flailing. Surprise registered in his eyes just as she clipped his jaw with a punch. He grunted in pain and in the next instant caught the left hook sailing his way. His fingers circled her wrist, brought her hand down and turned her around, tucking her body securely in front of his. He let go of her hand and wrapped both of his strong arms around her middle, holding her immobile.

They were both breathing hard from the fight. Josie struggled, but his muscular body and firm hold were no match for her. She felt trapped, weak and defenseless. And she hated that it was Seth O'Connor who provoked those vulnerable emotions.

He shifted his weight behind her, and she became all too aware of their intimate position...his broad chest pressing against her back and the way his pelvis tucked against her bottom.

She swallowed hard. She'd worn an old pair of cutoffs today, along with an equally old blouse she'd haphazardly knotted just beneath her unbound breasts to keep cool. Where his corded forearms were braced around her mid-section, her bare skin burned. The rough material of his jeans scratched the back of her thighs and the bend of her knee.

His face moved beside hers, and she could feel his warm breath brush across her cheek and flutter the wispy auburn strands that had escaped the hair she'd pinned up earlier, could feel a light stubble graze her jaw. And for a fleeting moment, his hold seemed to loosen as if he was cradling her in his arms.

A warm, masculine scent surrounded her, like earth, leather and sun all combined into one. Her stomach flut-tered and her breasts swelled and tightened. She gritted her teeth, hating herself for responding to him in any way but anger. He deserved nothing less than her contempt after the way he'd used her and deliberately broken her heart.

"Let me go," she muttered furiously.

His mouth moved to her ear. "Not so brave without your rifle, now are you, darlin'?" he taunted.

She closed her eyes against the sudden rush of tears surg-ing forward. "I hate you," she whispered, voicing the words that had been locked inside her for eleven painful years.

"Yeah, well, Josie darlin'," he said on a long, drawn-out sigh, "the feeling's completely mutual."

"Mom?"

The softly spoken word in a child's quivering voice served to do what Josie's demands could not. Seth imme-diately released her and straightened. Josie went to her daughter who had stopped in the doorway, her only thought to soothe her fears.

Josie smoothed Kellie's curly auburn hair, so much like her own, away from her stricken face. "It's okay, sweetie," she said gently, knowing the lie was necessary.

Peeking around her mother, Kellie eyed the large man standing on the porch. "Who is he?"

Josie pulled in a deep breath. "His name is Seth O'Connor."

Kellie frowned. "Is he one of those no-good O'Connor boys I've heard Grandpa talking about? Did you shoot him?"

Josie grimaced at her child's guileless questions. Although the McAllisters and O'Connors weren't on friendly terms by any stretch of the imagination, she'd raised her daughter to be nonjudgmental—and that included the McAllisters' nemesis.

"He's our neighbor, remember?" She'd explained as much when Kellie had first asked her who the O'Connors were—and that's all she'd told her daughter because that had been the only pleasant way to explain who Jay and Seth were. At the tender age of ten, Kellie didn't need to be privy to just how bitter their relationship was or how far back the O'Connors had hated the McAllisters. "And no, I didn't shoot him."

Josie looked back at Seth, giving him a direct, pointed stare as if to suggest she was beginning to regret that decision. "Mr. O'Connor was just leaving."

He crossed his arms over his chest, looking as formidable as a Brahman bull. "I'm not going anywhere until we talk."

She didn't understand him, his insistence, or his crazy talk about the Golden M being his property. But whatever he had to say, she didn't want it said in front of her daughter. Once again, she requested that Kellie go inside while she settled a few issues with Mr. O'Connor. Reluctantly, and with a few more assurances, the young girl obeyed.

Josie closed the door after her daughter as a precaution, then in a tone filled with feigned politeness, she said to Seth, "You may think you're here to talk, but we have nothing to say to one another."

His gaze flickered down the length of her, taking in her summertime attire with too obvious an interest. As if he was taking stock of her—like a cowboy sizing up a potential breeding mare. When his eyes reached hers again, they were filled with heated resentment.

"Polite talk, no," he agreed, his voice harsh. "But this is in regard to a business-related matter."

"Business?" She shook her head at the absurdity of the notion. "I wouldn't do business with an O'Connor if you were the last man on earth who could offer me sanctuary."

A faint smile curved his mouth. "I might just very well be."

Fed up with whatever game he was playing, she stared him down. "Get off my property." She directed her finger toward his horse to emphasize her point. *"Now!"*

He didn't budge, and there was enough smugness touching his features to make her uneasy. "Don't be so hasty, darlin'."

Her temper flared at his sweet talk. "Do I need to call the sheriff out to arrest you for trespassing, not to mention assault?"

"Assault?" His dark brows rose incredulously, right along with his voice. "You're the one who damn near blew my head off!"

She lifted her chin a defiant notch and gave him a cool smile. "I was feeling…threatened."

"Like hell you were!" He clamped his lips shut and glared. "If anybody is calling the sheriff, I am. I've got a deed that states the Golden M belongs to me."

"You're crazy!"

"I'm perfectly sane." He rocked back on his booted heels, looking altogether too pleased with himself. "Has your father been around lately?"

The casual way he asked the question, and the insinuation behind his words, put her on the alert. Her father had been gone for two days, since that past Friday, though this wasn't the first time Jake McAllister had taken off without warning. She'd grown used to her father's drifting and the fact that he'd lost interest in the ranch years ago. She'd been handling the business end of the Golden M for almost eight years now, and with Mac as their longtime foreman running the day-to-day cattle operation, the ranch was still thriving. Nothing grand, but she was paying their bills and keeping a roof over their heads and food on the table.

So why was Seth so interested in her father...and why was he spouting this nonsense about a deed to the Golden M? It *had* to be nonsense, or a ploy of some sort.

She tried to keep calm and not let the panic within her claw its way to the surface. That would never do, because someone as unscrupulous as Seth would take advantage of her weakness.

"My father's whereabouts are none of your business," she snapped.

He walked toward where she was standing and circled her, so close his arm brushed her bottom. Deliberately? she wondered. She suppressed the urge to give him a sharp jab in the ribs with her elbow. She refused to give him the satisfaction of knowing he'd rattled her.

He stopped in front of her. "Did you know your father has a penchant for gambling?" His tone was casual, but there was nothing nonchalant about what he was suggesting.

Josie's heart dropped to her stomach, and a peculiar sense of dread filled her. While Seth's father had been notorious for drinking and being loud and obnoxious, her own father had gained a reputation for being an easy gambler. He loved poker, could sniff a game five miles away. There were many times he'd start the game of cards himself in some back room in a seedy bar. Sometimes he was lucky; most times he was not. Bottom line, he was addicted to the game, to the point where she feared he'd sink the ranch into bankruptcy. So far, she'd been successful in thwarting every attempt he'd made to take out a second loan on the ranch, knowing he'd use that money to finance his gambling habit.

She moved away from Seth to the white banister enclosing the porch. Unable to meet his disconcerting stare, she looked out at the fertile land stretching for miles in front of her. Land that had been in her family for three generations. Land that had once belonged to an O'Connor. "What does my father's gambling have to do with anything?"

She heard one of the pair of wicker chairs behind her creak as he settled his weight into it. "Your father gambled away the Golden M, and I won it."

Josie's world tilted, and she grabbed one of the columns for balance. She glanced over her shoulder at him, denial pumping up her adrenaline. He sat there in the white wicker chair, his long body stretched out, his legs crossed at his boots, looking entirely too arrogant.

She pressed a hand to her churning stomach. God, this had to be an awful dream, a nightmare she'd wake up from and laugh about. But Seth was flesh-and-blood real, his persistence too intense to be anything but genuine.

"Prove it," she blurted, despising the desperation in her voice. But that's exactly how she was feeling, grasping at straws in hopes of finding a discrepancy in his outrageous claim.

Withdrawing a square piece of paper from his shirt pocket, he unfolded it, then handed it toward her. "Here's all the proof you're gonna need."

She stared at the proffered document for what seemed like an eternity, the words "Quitclaim Deed" swirling in front of her. With a trembling hand, she reached for the paper and forced herself to read the contents. She got as far as the statement transferring ownership of the property to Seth O'Connor before a wave of disbelief crashed through her.

"How can this be?" she asked, more to herself than him.

"It's all very simple," he said, his eyes dark and unfathomable. "Your father and I were at Joe's pub Friday night and he challenged me to a game of poker in the back room."

"And you took advantage of him?" she demanded to know.

Seth laughed, the sound deep and rich despite the tension between them. "I know you'd like to believe I did, but I wasn't the only one in the game. There were five of us present, but I seemed to be the one with all the luck. Your father lost all the cash he had on him and resorted to writing IOUs. At one point, he owed me over ten grand, and Gary Rial four grand."

Josie groaned, staggered at the debt her father had incurred. "What happened?" she asked, not sure she really wanted to know.

"It came down to my hand against his, and since he had another three grand of IOUs in the pot and was about to write another just to stay in the game, I struck a deal with him."

Her loathing gaze narrowed on him. "What kind of deal did my father make with the devil himself?"

He lifted a dark brow at her derogatory comment. "I told him if he put in the deed to the Golden M and he won the pot, I'd forgive his IOU to me and I'd pay off Gary's. The same would apply if he lost. Either way, he'd have no outstanding debts."

"My, wasn't that generous of you!" Her fingers curled tightly around the deed in her hand. A deed that made the very porch she stood on, the house and ranch she grew up on, *his*. The thought made her nauseous.

He sat up in the chair, his gaze holding hers steadily. "He didn't have to put in the deed, Josie."

"Doesn't sound like he had much of a choice."

Anger flashed in his eyes, hot and dangerous. "He made

every choice on his own. I offered a deal, and he accepted it with a stipulation of his own that I agreed to. If he wasn't prepared to lose, then he never should have challenged me to join the game in the first place.''

He was right, she knew. Her father's weakness was no one's fault but his own. Still, she wasn't going to lose everything that mattered to her without a battle. "I'm going to do everything in my power to get this ranch back.''

Slowly, he stood, looking entirely too sexy for someone she despised. "You can certainly try, but that document is legal and binding. Considering the ranch wasn't in *your* name, you won't have much of a leg to stand on.''

Her chest grew so tight it hurt to breathe. Oh, Lord! She'd never thought to change the deed to include her name, never believed her father could be so desperate as to risk their home in a poker game. She was the last McAllister, and the ranch would have been hers one day, passed on from father to daughter.

She found it ironic that Jake McAllister had lost the property to an O'Connor the same way her great-grandfather McAllister had won it from Seth's great-grandfather so long ago—in a poker game.

That had been the beginning of the McAllister and O'Connor feud. Judging by the animosity vibrating between the two of them, that dissension was still burning bright and strong. But there had been a brief time when she believed she and Seth would be the ones to end the conflicts that had trickled down through three generations. She'd been so hopeful that the strife between their families would finally be over.

She'd been young and naive, and so wrong about Seth O'Connor's intentions…so easily duped by a heart-stopping grin and so effortlessly seduced by the taste of her first real kiss and the promise of true love.

She was older now and certainly wiser about how the O'Connors operated. She'd learned the hard way their motives were always self-serving. With that thought, she hardened her resolve. "You won't get away with this, Seth," she vowed, and thrust the offending document back at him.

"I already have." Expression uncompromising, he took the deed from her. When his fingers brushed hers, she felt as though she'd been zapped by a bolt of lightning. The sizzle coursed up her arm, spread through her breasts and settled in the pit of her stomach like a warm pool of molasses.

She shook off the unwanted sensation and jutted her chin up a notch, refusing to be intimidated by his superior height or the intense heat blazing in the depths of his blue eyes. "If you expect me to pack up and leave without a fight, then you better think again."

"On the contrary, darlin'," he said, his smooth drawl at odds with the resentment she detected in his voice, "I fully expect you to stay."

Wariness pulsed through her with every heartbeat, making her feel like a cornered deer staring down the barrel of a rifle—with no means of escape. Was he tricking her somehow? Letting her believe that he wasn't going to take away the only home she and Kellie had ever had? "I...I don't understand."

"There's a stipulation to the deed," he said very carefully, as if he wanted her to understand what he was about to say. "A provision your father set and I agreed to before I won that last poker hand."

So, he'd made his own sacrifice to gain what he wanted—the property that once belonged to his family. She was certain whatever price he paid wasn't as great as her father's loss or her own dismal future. "What kind of stipulation?"

His smile was grim. "That we get married."

CHAPTER TWO

JOSIE stared at Seth incredulously. Losing the ranch to him was one thing, but to *marry* him? She knew her father could be irresponsible, but she couldn't imagine him making such a ridiculous demand, and an O'Connor, no less so.

"You're joking!" He *had* to be.

"I wish I was." He crossed his arms over his wide chest, his mouth twisting into a sardonic smile. "The stipulation states that I'll marry you within one week in order to gain the Golden M."

The way she saw it, if she refused her father's terms, there was no way Seth could claim the property. Her father had outsmarted an O'Connor!

It was her turn to be smug. "What makes you believe I'd *want* to marry you to fulfill the terms of that stipulation?"

"Because it would be in *both* our interests to do so."

He didn't look the least bit concerned by her unwillingness to help him carry out the terms of her father's stipulation, and that realization caused a niggling of unease to curl within her. "How do you figure it would be in *my* best interest to marry someone I despise just so he could claim my property?"

A hint of challenge flickered in his gaze. "Because if you don't become my wife, you forfeit the Golden M."

She frowned at him. "That doesn't make any sense."

From his shirt pocket where he'd tucked away the quit-claim deed, he now withdrew another folded piece of paper. Opening it, he held it toward her.

"Read the terms of the stipulation for yourself," he prompted when she merely stared at the signed and notarized document. "It states that I'll marry you within a week in order to procure the Golden M, at which time it will become joint property since we'll be man and wife." He gave her a moment to absorb that before continuing. "However, if you refuse to marry me within the specified week, then you lose the Golden M and I'll have every right as the owner to toss you off the ranch. And if we do get married and one of us insists upon a divorce, that person forfeits their half of the land to the other."

Unable to believe her father would enforce such binding conditions, she grabbed the document from him and read the contents. By the time she verified her father's signature on the bottom line, panic and dread had balled in her stomach.

She stared up at Seth, tasting the bitterness of defeat. "You agreed to this…to this farce?"

"I've got nothing to lose." He casually moved closer, and her heart rate accelerated. "And a whole lot to gain."

She was the one who'd have to relinquish everything if she balked at the terms outlined in the agreement. It just didn't make sense. Why would her father force her to marry someone who hated her as equally as she detested him, then set forth terms that made a future divorce nearly impossible unless she walked away from the only home she'd ever known?

"So, what'll it be, Josie darlin'?" he asked, his voice dropping to a low, husky pitch. Reaching out, he stroked his knuckles over her cheek, the tender gesture at odds with the fierce light in his eyes. "Shall I make an appointment with Reverend Wilcox for this week?"

She opened her mouth to make a scathing response but found her throat suddenly dry. His thumb brazenly skimmed over her bottom lip as softly as a butterfly's caress. Her stomach dipped and tumbled. Bolder still, he held her gaze and strummed his warm fingers down her throat and along the open collar of her blouse.

Her breathing deepened and she shivered, unable to stop the memories of how gentle those big hands of his could be as they slid over her body. How delightfully sweet and seductive.

It had been so long since she'd experienced such consuming passion, such awesome need...but it all came crashing back to her in that moment. She couldn't help the tiny moan that escaped her.

Seth watched her with great interest, a faint, satisfied smile touching his mouth. "Seems to me there could be other advantages to our getting married," he murmured as one long finger slowly followed the V of her blouse to where the last button ended between her breasts.

Her nipples automatically tightened, and she knew he could see the dusky rose tips through the thin cotton material. Horrified that he could manipulate her emotions so easily and still have so much control over her body's response to him, she reached for her temper, embraced the flood of anger and let it explode.

She slapped his hand away from the button she knew he could so easily flick open with his fingers—he'd proved that particular skill eleven years ago. "I'll see you in hell before I agree to marry you!"

She tried to move around him, but he was fast and agile, bracing both his hands on the porch railing on either side of her, trapping her against him. Before she could raise her knee and use it as a means of self-defense, he pushed a hard thigh between hers, immobilizing her lower body.

The heat that flared within her matched the flames in his eyes. She shoved at his shoulders, but he was a solid mass of muscle and strength, and the only thing her struggling accomplished was to make Seth press closer. Their position became as intimate as two lovers entwined in a sensual embrace.

Except they were enemies and hated one another. She

doubted Seth found anything arousing about their situation. She certainly didn't!

She attempted to lean back, but the railing bit into her spine. That discomfort was nothing compared to the scratch of denim between her thighs and the metallic bite of Seth's heavy belt buckle pressing against the strip of bare skin exposed between her breasts and the waistband of her shorts. She did her best to ignore the liquid warmth rushing through her veins.

He blew out a harsh breath that tickled the loose strands of hair around her face. His body shifted subtly to accommodate her wriggling, and she felt the muscles flex beneath the hands she'd flattened on his chest. She was appalled to discover that he wasn't as immune to their position as she'd originally thought. The evidence of his desire nudged the front zipper of her shorts, an unmistakable masculine hardness that caused a deep, clenching thrill to spiral straight to where his knee pressed so insistently.

She didn't understand how two people who despised each other so much could respond to one another on such a primitive, sensual level. Couldn't comprehend how eleven years of anger and hurt could melt away with just a look, a touch from Seth. He seemed to be her greatest weakness despite his past betrayal.

His warm gaze focused on her mouth, and the vital hunger she saw there swept through her like the heat of wildfire. And then he gradually lowered his head, his parted lips homing in on hers.

She couldn't breathe. Couldn't move. She was fully aware of the quiver of anticipation thrumming beneath the surface of her skin, the need to give herself to this man she'd never been able to forget...or forgive.

Summoning every ounce of willpower she possessed, she turned her head away just as his lips descended. His mouth landed on her cheek, warm and damp and soft as down. Her lack of cooperation didn't succeed in hindering the rogue's exploration. His lips slid along her jaw to her ear, and she thought he murmured, "You still want me as much as I want you," but couldn't be sure. His rich, dark voice rumbled along her nerve endings, making it impossible for her to think coherently...making her dizzy with a wanting that was not only stupid, but dangerous.

She gritted her teeth against the onslaught of his blatant sexuality and her body's shocking response to his seduction tactics. "I hate you," she whispered hoarsely, reminding him, and herself, of that fact. "And I refuse to marry you."

Finally, he lifted his head and gave her the breathing room she so desperately needed, but he didn't let her loose. Triumph shone in his dark, sexy eyes. "You'd give me the ranch so easily? Just because you can't stand the thought of me being your husband and having the right to touch you and kiss you? Or is it because you can't stand the fact that you *want* me to touch you and kiss you that has you so fired up?"

His words were mocking, too accurate, and they enraged her. His hold slackened, along with his body, giving her enough room to pull her arm back and wallop him in the belly. He grunted at the impact, but she knew the punch had startled him more than hurt him. Reflexively, he moved his arms from the railing to defend himself, enabling her to take advantage of his surprise and escape. Sidestepping him, she headed down the porch stairs and headed across the lawn toward the stables in her bare feet. She came upon the Stetson she'd shot off his head earlier. Smirking at the gaping hole in the crown, she gave it a good swift kick that sent it tumbling in the opposite direction.

She heard him swear colorfully from behind her and ignored him when he demanded she come back so they could finish their discussion. His boots echoed off the wooden steps as he followed her. She picked up her pace, putting as much distance as she could between them, even though she knew it was inevitable they talk and settle issues.

His taunting words, *You'd give me the ranch so easily?*, played through her mind, making her realize the seriousness of her quandary. No, she wouldn't just hand over the only home she'd ever known. But the thought of becoming Seth O'Connor's wife and living with him on a daily basis with all the resentment and bitterness between them was enough to make her want to rail at the injustice.

There was Kellie to consider in this mess of things, too. How would her daughter react to her mother's marrying a virtual stranger? And most importantly, how would Seth treat Kellie, considering the awful rumors of the past?

Dad, how could you do this to me? Tears of frustration and uncertainty burned the back of her eyes. She needed to find her father—not that his presence would change the future if those documents Seth had in his possession were legal. But surely they could work out some other compromise or monetary compensation.

He caught her before she could slip into the stables and lose him in the maze of stalls. His hand closed around her arm, bringing her to an abrupt halt, and he turned her around to face him. She glared at his intrusion, despite the hot tears of anger threatening to spill over her lashes.

One look into her eyes and the dark, irritable scowl etching his features slowly faded, replaced by something more charitable. Compassion? she briefly wondered. Surely not. An O'Connor wouldn't know that emotion if it slapped him in the face.

"Look," he said, his tone gruff with impatience, "I know this is a shock and you're upset—"

"I'm not upset. I'm *furious!*" She shook off his hand, her lips pursing into a tight line. "This is *my* home, and I'll be damned if I'll just hand it over to you without a fight!"

"If you fight, you'll lose everything, Josie," he stated relentlessly. "Thanks to your father, there's one way you can win and keep the ranch and land, and that's to marry me.''

She laughed, but the sound was dry and humorless. "Yes, it was quite thoughtful of my father to add that stipulation, but it's hard to be grateful when I can't stand the thought of being married to you."

His jaw tightened at her barb. "You're not my first choice of a bride, either."

Resurrected anger and hurt shimmered between them. She saw the animosity of the past in his eyes, felt the misery in her heart. Once, she'd wanted to marry him, but that had been before she realized that his interest had nothing to do with love and everything to do with simple revenge on a McAllister.

"Then why did you agree to my father's terms?" she asked, keeping their conversation, and her thoughts, firmly entrenched in the present. "Why didn't you just let him lose the money and let the IOUs stand? I would have found a way to pay you and Gary back."

The corner of his mouth tipped in an easy smile, reminding her how charming he could be. "You always were the responsible one of the family, weren't you?"

She stiffened, recalling how she'd confided in him when she was sixteen, how she'd foolishly opened her heart and revealed things she'd never told anyone before. She'd told Seth about how her mother died when she was just a little girl of five, and how something in her father died, too, casting him adrift. As a young girl, she'd struggled to keep the household together and, with Mac's help, learned everything she needed to know about running the ranch until she was finally old enough to take over for her wandering father.

But Seth already knew most of that, and she was beyond needing a shoulder to cry on. "Answer my question," she said. "If you didn't like my father's terms, which include marrying me, why didn't you just let my father lose the money and let the IOUs stand?''

"It's not the money I'm after, Josie." Sighing, he transferred his gaze to the green pasture next to the stables. Something in his expression softened as he looked out over the land that went on for miles. "I want this spread, partly because it was originally O'Connor land."

"Partly?" she questioned, guessing there was more and wanting to hear it all. "What's the other reason?"

Meeting her gaze again, he pushed his fingers through his thick hair, disheveling the strands more than they already were. "I want a place of my own—"

"You have a place of your own," she interrupted heatedly. "You have the Paradise Wild!"

"Jay inherited Paradise Wild when my father died four years ago."

She couldn't contain her shock. "Your father didn't leave the place to the both of you?"

"Nope," he said, his tone filled with a bitterness she didn't understand. "I just work the ranch and live in a cabin on Jay's property. He shares the house with his wife and two kids."

She couldn't help but wonder what had happened for David O'Connor to disinherit his younger son.

Seth must have sensed the questions forming in her mind since he quickly diverted them. "I agreed to Jake's terms because as much as I want this ranch and property, I have no desire to leave you and your daughter homeless. Marrying you is a small price for me to pay to gain this land."

She refused to give up so easily. "Let me give you the money my father and Gary owed you, and a little more for your trouble, and leave us alone. I'll give you enough to put a down payment on another spread."

He shook his head. "I can't do that."

"Can't, or won't?" Desperation made her voice rise a few decibels.

"Both," he said in a tone that brooked no compromise. "This was O'Connor land before it ever belonged to a McAllister, and now it's back in the family. And even then, we don't know the legitimacy of a McAllister winning it in a poker game all those years ago."

"My great-grandfather won this land fair and square," she said, unable to believe any McAllister would cheat so ruthlessly. "And now you're getting everything we McAllisters worked so hard to build from nothing more than dirt and barren land."

Her arguments didn't sway him in the least. "I'm not giving up the deed, Josie, so resign yourself to the fact that there is only one way for you to keep this ranch."

Her hopes began to dwindle. "And that's to marry you?"

"Yes." His expression held no apology or remorse. "I'm willing to put our differences aside and make the marriage work. I'm even willing to take full responsibility for your daughter, even though she's someone else's child."

"How gracious," she said, nearly choking on the words. "But that's not necessary. Kellie is nobody's responsibility but my own. She's lived ten years without a father and managed just fine." Josie could see curious questions in Seth's eyes regarding her daughter and knew she wasn't prepared to answer any of them. "You've conducted your business, and now I'd appreciate it if you'd leave."

"In a minute," he said, and from the back pocket of his jeans brought out a folded envelope and handed it to her. "When I picked up the deed from your father's attorney, he asked me to give you this letter that Jake left for you."

Not about to refuse the only link she might have to her father, she took the envelope from him.

"Think about your options carefully, Josie, and I'll be

back in a few days for your answer." He turned and headed for the stables where he'd left his horse. She watched him mount the chestnut in a fluid motion, then direct the mare around to face her.

His horse pranced anxiously, champing at the bit to go. Seth effortlessly held the powerful horse in check with a slight pressure of his thighs. From atop his steed, Seth perused the length of her one last time, from her springy auburn curls, past the blouse tied beneath her breasts, over her faded cutoffs to the tips of her bare toes. By the time he finished his blatant male survey, her pulse was racing out of control and she felt more restlessly inflamed than she cared to admit.

I hate him, she mentally chanted, and shook off the disturbing sensations unfurling within her.

He smiled as if reading her thoughts and accepting her challenge. "Keep in mind, Josie darlin'," he said, reverting back to that sexy, lazy drawl of his, "we'll need to be married by next Friday, or everything is mine."

On that last parting shot, he took off, spurring his horse across McAllister land that eventually gave way to O'Connor property, leaving Josie behind to make a decision that would either bind her to a man who'd cruelly deceived her or force her to give up the only home she and Kellie had ever known.

Either way, she saw heartache in her future.

Seth rode his horse hard and fast toward Paradise Wild, but no matter how ruthlessly he pushed Lexi for speed, he found he couldn't outrun his conflicting feelings for the woman he'd just left behind.

He slowed Lexi as they neared a wide creek that trickled down from the mountain butting against the side of McAllister and O'Connor property. He waited until his mare had settled, then slid out of the saddle and dropped the reins so she could graze.

Bending down by the creek, he scooped the cool, clear liquid into his palm, brought it to his mouth and quenched his thirst. Then he dipped both hands into the water and ran them through his hair, slicking the thick strands away from his face.

Damn Josie and her trigger-happy finger anyway, he thought irritably. That had been his favorite Stetson, shaped perfectly to his head after years of use, and now he was going to have to break in a new one.

Sighing heavily, he stared at his scowling expression reflecting off the crystalline water. He wanted to hate her just as she claimed to despise him. And for eleven years he'd been able to believe that Josie McAllister meant nothing to him, that their brief time together in high school had been a grave mistake and taught him a valuable lesson he'd never forgotten. Like not to trust a McAllister's motives.

But try as he might, he never could forget Josie. No matter how many women he'd dated over the years, he couldn't wipe out the memories of how silky and warm her skin had felt beneath his hands, the sweet taste of her lips, her light, lilting laughter, and especially the soft sounds of pleasure she made when he'd slid deep inside her body. Those images had haunted him every night since the last time they'd made love.

The connection between them had seemed magical, considering they'd been taught all their lives to hate the other. During grade school he'd ridiculed her mercilessly, taking his cue from his older brother, Jay. As a young boy, he remembered that he hadn't liked hurting Josie with those nasty taunts, but Jay had wanted to keep the rift fueled any way he could, and whenever he suggested they leave her alone, Jay would make his life miserable until he proved that he could dole out his share of jeers and mean insults.

Seth shook his head at the immaturity of his youth, more than a little disgusted that his own father had encouraged the dissension between the McAllister girl and his own boys.

That familial pressure ebbed when Jay finally graduated high school, leaving Seth as a senior and Josie as a sophomore. By that time, she was taking great pains to avoid him, not that he could blame her after the way he and his brother had treated her. When by chance they passed in the halls or on the campus, she never looked him in the eye. He didn't know why, but he didn't like the thought of her believing he was as rotten as his brother.

One day as she walked out of a classroom, he'd literally slammed into her, so hard that the impact knocked her back on her bottom and the books in her arms flew in five different directions. She'd sat there frozen, with her skirt up around her thighs, staring at him with a panic-stricken look on her face. Just like an animal cornered by a hunter, waiting for him to either shoot or let her go free.

He remembered thinking how pretty she was, with wild curly hair the hue of fire and cinnamon, wide green eyes emphasized by dark brows, and the smattering of freckles over the bridge of her nose. And he couldn't help but notice those shapely legs of hers and the small, firm breasts beneath her clingy T-shirt—her blossoming curves were what boys his age fantasized about.

And in that moment, he felt as though he'd been struck by lightning. His heart thudded erratically in his chest and his palms grew damp. It was a crazy feeling, one he'd never experienced before.

Clearing his dry throat, he squatted to her level and handed her the biology book that had landed by his sneakered foot. "Are you all right?" he'd asked.

Not sparing him the slightest glance, she scrambled to collect her other books. "I'm f-f-fine," she'd said in a soft, quivering voice.

She stood, and just as she attempted to dart around him, he caught her arm. Immediately, she stopped and stiffened, as if she feared he'd rip off her limb if she didn't. Her body began to tremble as she waited.

"I'm sorry," he said gently, not for bumping into her, but for all the years of torment he and his brother had put her through.

"I, uh, should have, um—" she swallowed back the tears he heard in her voice, the same ones he saw pooling in her eyes "—watched where I was g-g-going."

Before he could explain what he'd meant, she wrenched her arm away and fled down the corridor and out the doors leading to the front of the school. He should have let things end there but found he couldn't. He followed her home from school, and when he was positive they were alone, he approached her as she entered the woods that lined both of their properties.

This time, she didn't cower. Fire flashed in her eyes and she dropped her schoolbooks on the ground. She told him she was tired of being bullied, then came at him full force in an attempt to defend herself. Her attack knocked them both to the moss-covered ground, him on his back, with her sprawled on top of him.

Eyes closed, he didn't move a muscle, not wanting to threaten her in any way, though the press of her lithe body along his conjured up some interesting fantasies. He began mentally reciting his times tables to detach himself from the situation until his randier thoughts settled.

She squirmed on top of him, her breasts brushing across his chest as she propped herself up on her elbows to look down at him. "Oh, my gosh!" she exclaimed, worry in her voice.

Six times seven is forty-two.

She sat up, straddling his lower body so her thighs bracketed his hips, and gently cupped his face in her cool hands. "Seth?" He decided he liked the way his name sounded on her lips. "Seth, are you okay?"

He wanted to groan at the exquisite feel of her bottom

tucked so intimately against him but found he couldn't utter a sound. *Six times eight is forty-eight.*

Her fingers quickly unbuttoned his shirt and her palm slid inside, right over his heart. "You're not breathing!"

He wasn't? Then why was he so aware of that intense heat pooling low in his belly and his body's embarrassing reaction to Josie's position? He concentrated on his arithmetic. *Six times nine is fifty-four.*

"I didn't really mean to kill you." She moved off him, her tone frantic. "I swear I didn't!" Tilting his head back, she pinched his nose closed and pressed her mouth to his.

He felt her soft lips on his and believed he'd died and gone to heaven. Air whooshed into his lungs, *her very breath*, and he began to cough and gulp more air. Finally, wheezing in a breath, his eyes opened.

"Oh, Seth," she cried in obvious relief, "you're okay!"

It took him a moment to realize what had happened and reorient himself. "I think you just knocked the breath out of me."

And there, in the woods, it happened...a spark of awareness Seth decided to nurture, with her cooperation, of course. He'd gently cupped the back of her head and brought her mouth back to his and kissed her like he'd been wanting to ever since he'd bumped into her in the hall. Her lips parted beneath the subtle pressure of his, and she moaned deep in her throat, but the sound wasn't one of alarm. No, she didn't fear him. She sank against his chest, closed her eyes and let his tongue explore her mouth and tempt her to join in the slow, drugging kiss.

At nearly eighteen, he was two years older than her, had been on plenty of dates and kissed a lot of girls. But none of them tasted as sweet as Josie. He couldn't get enough of her, and it seemed she was just as needy.

From that day on, he met her after school, anxious to be with her. Because neither of them wanted their families to know they were seeing one another for fear of repercussions, he met her at the edge of the woods and spent as much time with her as possible until they had to head home. Eventually, kisses weren't enough, and he'd coaxed her to make love. They'd been good together, her uninhibited response to his touch driving him wild with desire for her. He'd been careful about protecting her, but three months later she tearfully informed him she was pregnant.

He'd been scared, certain his father would flay him alive—that's how much David O'Connor loathed the McAllisters. So, instead, he'd confided in his brother.

"How do you know it's your baby?" Jay had asked him.

His brother's question made him wary. "What the hell are you talking about?" he demanded to know.

Jay smirked. "Considering she's slept with half the senior class, there's no telling whose brat it is."

He'd been so furious with his brother's claim he'd given Jay a black eye. A few days later, the rumors started circulating around school, and he heard bragging in the locker room about Josie and other boys. Considering he'd used protection every time they'd slept together, he found the claims difficult to ignore.

Josie, it seemed, had manipulated him for her own purposes. If she meant to dupe an O'Connor, she'd nearly succeeded. She'd put on a flawless act, making him believe he was the first and only one to know her intimately. The thought had filled him with a white-hot fury and made him plan a fitting retribution.

He saw her one last time. She'd expected him to marry her, to give her bastard child the O'Connor name. Instead of the proposal she anticipated, he'd coldly informed her that he'd deliberately seduced her to gain revenge on the McAllisters, and she'd fallen for the ruse. And since at least a dozen other guys could be the baby's father, she was on her own.

She'd appeared so convincingly devastated, he'd had to steel himself against the hurt glittering in her tear-filled eyes. Her pain and despair had seemed so terribly real. But not once did she deny the awful rumors. Not once did she try to explain. She'd walked away from him, head held high.

He hadn't talked to her since, hadn't been close enough to touch her...until today. And damned if he still didn't want her with the same fierceness of his youth, and that irked him more than he cared to admit.

Seth scrubbed a hand over his jaw and let out a low growl of frustration. He hadn't anticipated her seductive allure, the way her body had filled out with lush, womanly curves that tempted and teased a man's interest. She was an exciting blend of fire and spirit, and that fiery disposition of hers made him burn hotter than any of the demure, accommodating women he'd dated over the years.

Gruff laughter escaped him. After eleven years of trying to pretend Josie McAllister didn't exist for him, he found it ironic that he was going to marry her. He didn't doubt that once her temper cooled she'd agree to become his wife. Despite her fury over her father's gambling loss, he was certain marrying him was the lesser of two evils when it came to giving up the Golden M. And marrying Josie was a small sacrifice on his part for gaining a prosperous piece of land to call his own.

Seth stood and headed toward his mare. He needed to tell Jay about this recent turn of events and let him know he'd be short a hand and would need to hire someone to replace him. He dreaded the discussion to come, suspecting that Jay was going to explode when he learned that a McAllister was about to become a part of their family. Jay blamed the McAllisters for every misfortune they'd ever encountered. In Seth's opinion, which he'd always been smart enough to keep to himself, their family's misfortune was a direct result of mismanagement and too much resentment. He supposed it was easier to blame the family's old adversary than face the truth that their father hadn't cared enough to nurture the fertile land they'd lived on, choosing instead to spend his time at the local bar, which had left him drunk and in a surly disposition more often than not.

Refusing to dwell on the bitterness of the past, and the fact that his own father had disinherited him for reasons that proved how spiteful and unforgiving David O'Connor could be, Seth mounted his horse, determined to keep a clear focus on his future—which included Josie as his wife and the Golden M as his new home.

Turning Lexi north, he headed toward Paradise Wild and the unpleasant task ahead.

CHAPTER THREE

SETH found his brother in the spacious office located in the back of the main stable. The door was open, but since Jay seemed engrossed in the open journal on his desk and hadn't heard him enter the building, he knocked on the wooden frame so he didn't startle him.

Jay glanced up, wire-rimmed reading glasses framing his hazel eyes. "Where have you been?" he asked, his tone tinged with a hint of annoyance. "You missed Sunday dinner."

"Sorry 'bout that." Usually he was courteous enough to let Jay's wife, Erin, know when he wasn't going to be around for breakfast, dinner or supper so she didn't prepare extra and they didn't wait on him. Though Seth lived in one of the two cabins located on the ranch, eating with Jay's family was part of his wages as a hand. It worked for him, considering what a lousy cook he was. "I didn't think I'd be as long as I was."

Jay's gaze flickered over his tousled hair, noted the absence of his Stetson, then narrowed speculatively. "I noticed Lexi was gone. You out checking fences or something? If so, you know you don't get paid for working Sundays."

"I wasn't working," Seth assured his brother, tamping down the spurt of bitterness surging to the surface. He hated being treated like an employee on the very land that should have been half his. He wanted to believe he'd gotten over his father's slight, but there were times, like now, when he felt the lash of David O'Connor's punishment straight to the core. "I was over at the McAllister place."

That snagged his brother's attention. He closed the journal in front of him and pushed it aside. "Doing what?" he asked tentatively.

Drawing out the moment of victory, Seth folded his frame into the dark brown Naugahyde chair in front of Jay's desk, making himself comfortable. "I was claiming the Golden M, which I won in a poker game against Jake McAllister."

It took a few extra seconds for the importance of his statement to sink in. Seth knew the exact moment it registered—when selfish retribution glittered in Jay's eyes. "No kidding? You won the Golden M?"

"Lock, stock and barrel," Seth confirmed. Prime cattle, fertile land, and a feisty woman who hated him enough to threaten his life with a rifle. All his in the span of one night, he thought wryly.

"Whooee!" Jay slapped a hand on the surface of his desk, a wide, gleeful grin splitting his face. "If that isn't poetic justice, I don't know what is."

"Yeah, it's ironic all right," he agreed mildly, "considering how we lost the land so long ago."

Leaning back in his squeaky chair, Jay began spouting plans for Seth's windfall. "We can join the property again, combine the livestock—"

"No." Every muscle in Seth's body had coiled tight.

Jay looked taken aback by Seth's refusal. His brows snapped together, emphasizing his displeasure. "What do you mean, 'no'?"

"The Golden M is *mine*, Jay." His tone was low, undeniably firm, and a trifle dangerous. "And it'll remain separate property."

"Why?" Jay challenged. Standing abruptly, he braced his hands flat on his desk and leaned toward Seth, glaring. "That's O'Connor property! It always has been. It should remain in the family as a whole."

Under normal circumstances, Seth would have agreed. But considering he'd been stripped of his rightful inheritance, he wasn't about to share what now belonged to him. "It hasn't been in our family for over seventy-five years. There's no reason why it needs to be part of Paradise Wild again."

Jay's mouth thinned in anger. "So, you'll be competing directly against me, then?"

"I'll be competing with no one but myself. You've got a fine breed of cattle, and there are plenty of buyers to accommodate both you and me."

"I can't believe this!" Jay's temper exploded and his face turned a bright shade of red. "Dad is probably rolling over in his grave right about now!"

"Probably, considering he left me with nothing, and I've acquired what he always wanted."

A sneer curled the corner of his brother's mouth. "If you wanted half of Paradise Wild, then you never should have messed around with Josie McAllister."

"You're right, of course," Seth graciously conceded to what had been the single most stupid mistake of his life. His brief affair with Josie had cost him so much...a chunk of his youthful pride, his half of Paradise Wild and the inability to give any other woman what he'd given her. His heart.

Refusing to dwell on past mistakes, he casually added, "Just so you know, I'll be marrying Josie by the end of the week."

Jay's eyes nearly bugged right out of their sockets. "*What*?" he wheezed.

A satisfied smile quirked Seth's mouth, and he decided that he enjoyed having the upper hand for a change. Very concisely, he explained the stipulation Jake McAllister had added to the deed to the Golden M, which included offering his daughter the benefit of marriage in order for her and his granddaughter to remain on the ranch.

Jay's blistering curses filled the office, and he paced the

length of space behind his desk. "And you actually agreed to those outrageous terms?"

Refusing to be baited, Seth shrugged nonchalantly. "I'd be a fool not to. I want the Golden M."

Jay stopped his agitated pacing and whirled to face Seth. His stare turned hard and bitter. "Yeah, you're a fool all right. An idiotic fool for marrying that little tra—"

"Don't say it," Seth interrupted, the chilling tone of his voice menacing enough to make Jay reconsider his derogatory remark. He stood and faced his brother squarely. He was taller than Jay by at least three inches and more muscular from the physical labor of working the ranch and herding cattle.

Now he used that superior strength to send a silent but unmistakable warning. "In fact, I'd appreciate it from here on that you keep any insulting comments about Josie to yourself." As much as Seth had his own personal grudges with Josie, he wouldn't tolerate his brother, or anyone else for that matter, slandering the woman who would be his wife.

"Good God, Seth," Jay breathed incredulously, "you're not still hot for her, are you?"

Oh, Josie made him plenty hot all right—in ways that her becoming his wife would certainly appease. "She's a means to an end," he said, stating a fact. "However, since she'll be my wife, I'll expect you to give her the same respect you would any other woman I would have married."

Jay shook his head, his eyes wide and wild, as if he was searching for a way to make Seth see reason. "Are you totally and completely out of your mind? You can't marry a *McAllister*!" He spit the word out like an expletive.

If Seth wasn't on the verge of letting his own anger get the best of him, he would have found his brother's ire amusing. But he didn't care for the ominous slant of their conversation or the hostility burning in Jay's gaze. For crying out loud, it wasn't as though *Jay* had to marry Josie.

He let out a deep breath that did nothing to ease the tense muscles in his body. "I *can* marry a McAllister, and I *will*." His brusque tone left no room for debate. "I suggest you get used to the idea."

Jay raked him with a scathing look. "You're going to marry her even after what she did to you?"

Seth didn't want to think about Josie's deceit, knowing if he dwelled on that aspect of their time together it would eat him alive. "What happened in the past has nothing to do with the present." Josie was a business deal, part of the package for the Golden M, which he wanted so badly he could taste the sweetness of freedom owning his own place would provide.

"She used you, Seth!" Jay pointed an angry finger his way for emphasis but didn't dare actually jab Seth with the offending digit. "And she tried to pawn off that brat of hers as yours after sleeping with God-only-knows how many guys!"

Seth's jaw clenched. Unbidden, visions of Josie's daughter filled his mind, momentarily taking the edge off his rising temper. The timid young girl looked just like Josie, with curly auburn hair and big green eyes. Nothing about her physical appearance gave any indication as to who her father could have been. Seth wondered if *Josie* even knew who'd fathered Kellie.

Shoving the disturbing thought out of his mind, he decided then and there that he wouldn't punish the girl for her mother's past indiscretions. It just wasn't fair.

He headed toward the door, ready to end their discussion, but paused in the threshold to glance back at Jay. He leveled his steady gaze on his brother, who looked absolutely livid at the turn of events. "That 'brat' is going to be *my* stepdaughter and *your* niece. I'll expect you to treat her with the same kindness I give your own two children, or you'll answer to me." With that, Seth left the office and headed down the long corridor to the entrance of the stable.

"Don't expect me to be at the wedding!" Jay yelled furiously after him.

Seth shook his head. He hadn't realized until that moment how his brother's spiteful attitude was so much like their father's. David O'Connor hadn't cut anyone any slack, especially not a McAllister, and he'd allowed old resentments to fester until it had totally consumed his life. Jay was on that same collision course, straight to emotional destruction.

And there wasn't a damn thing Seth could do about it.

As he walked out of the stables and felt the warmth of the sun on his face, Seth had the invigorating thought that he was no longer under his brother's thumb, no longer an employee of the Paradise Wild.

He grinned. He was a free man with a spread of his own.

And it felt pretty damn good.

The heartache was already beginning, starting with the letter Josie's father had left for her.

Sitting on the wooden bench just outside the barn, she read the brief correspondence Jake had scrawled on a scratch piece of paper. She read his words over and over, trying to understand why he'd risk the Golden M in a poker game, add an outrageous stipulation that would ruin her life and bind her to Seth O'Connor, when he knew there was every chance of losing to the last man in Montana she would have chosen for a husband.

But there were no answers in his letter. Just verification that the deed and stipulation were indeed real and binding and an apology for what he'd done, for failing her and letting his gambling addiction force him to resort to desperate measures, though he'd done his best to secure her future. He knew she'd be disappointed in him, angry even, and he couldn't bear to face her condemnation, so he'd decided it was best if he left. The note ended by saying that he hoped she'd finally find happiness and not hate him too much for what he'd done, and that he loved her and Kellie.

There was nothing about his returning, and that tore her up more than anything because she couldn't stand the thought of never seeing her father again.

The hot tears welling in her eyes finally spilled over her lashes. Tears because she would miss her father. Tears because she was so afraid of what her future would hold.

"Oh, Dad," she whispered around the ache in her heart. She was upset, yes. But she could never, ever spurn him despite the fact that he'd sold her soul to the devil himself. Together, they could have figured a way out of this mess. Alone, she had no way of defending herself from someone as formidable as Seth. He wanted the Golden M, and he wanted it badly enough to marry her for it.

Oh, what a doozy fate had delivered! If she wasn't so devastated, she would have been laughing hysterically at the twist.

She heard the screen door to the house slam shut and glanced up to see Kellie heading across the yard. She stopped and picked up Seth's hat, paused briefly to consider the hole in the crown, then continued toward the barn, carrying Josie's trophy with her.

Quickly, Josie wiped away the wetness on her cheeks and reached deep inside for some much needed fortitude to explain what changes lay ahead. She had to be strong for Kellie's sake because she was all her daughter had.

The little girl stopped in front of Josie, a frown creasing her delicately shaped brows. "He made you cry," she accused.

Her daughter looked so fiercely protective, Josie couldn't help but smile. "No, Mr. O'Connor didn't make me cry." She'd come close a few times, out of frustration and fury, but these tears had been for the man who'd raised her so lovingly. A man she feared they would never see again.

Kellie didn't look convinced. "What did that O'Connor man want?"

Our land. Our house. Everything I've worked so hard to nurture over the years.

She patted the space beside her on the bench. "Sit down, sweetie. We need to talk."

"I don't want to sit." The stubborn thrust of her chin didn't do much to mask the more uncertain emotions Josie saw hovering in her daughter's eyes.

Not wanting to upset Kellie any more than she had to, she stood and forced a bright smile that felt as phony as it probably looked. "Okay," she said easily. "Then how about we go for a walk?"

Taking Seth's ruined hat from her, Josie set it on the empty bench. Without waiting for another refusal, she draped a comforting arm around Kellie's shoulders and started walking along the white fence bordering the west pasture.

There was no easy way to broach the subject, so she just jumped right into the middle of it. "How do you feel about having a dad?"

"What do you mean?" Kellie asked skeptically.

Josie threaded her fingers through her daughter's sun-warmed hair. She loved this child so much, wanted so much more for her than she was about to give her—like a dad who would love her unconditionally. She didn't know if Seth was capable of accepting her daughter without past resentments and rumors getting in the way.

"Well, you've asked me before why I don't get married so you can have a dad," Josie said, trying to sound optimistic and cheerful. "And I was just wondering if you still felt the same way."

Kellie's slim shoulders lifted in a reserved shrug. "Yeah, I guess I do."

She closed her eyes for a few extra seconds, ignored the dread churning within her and just let it out. "Well, Mr. O'Connor and I are going to get married."

Kellie jerked away from her, her expression horrified. "But I don't want *him* as a dad! He's mean!"

Josie realized she had the choice of agreeing wholeheartedly with Kellie and tainting her daughter's perception of Seth right from the get-go, or she could make this transition for Kellie as smooth as possible. She might not like Seth, but there was no reason for Kellie to fear or hate him so vehemently.

The dirt drive had given way to a grassy knoll with patches of wildflowers. Josie stopped before they strolled too far away from the house and reached for her daughter's small hand, giving it a reassuring squeeze.

"Mr. O'Connor really isn't so bad." In fact, at one time he'd been charming and sweet, but that had all been a ploy. "When he came over today, he was upset, and so was I. The Golden M is his now, and in order for us to stay here, I have to marry him."

"Oh." Josie's explanation seemed to pacify her daughter and chase away the worry in her gaze. Kellie tilted her head, regarding Josie speculatively. "Do you love him?" she asked quietly.

The unexpected question knocked Josie for a loop, considering she'd once given Seth her heart and a piece of her soul. Thank goodness the fence was right behind her because she found she needed it for support. Once she'd regained her composure and calmed the erratic beating of her heart, she said very firmly, "No, I don't love him."

"But maybe someday you will?" Kellie asked expectantly.

Not likely, but she found she couldn't crush her daughter's simple hope for a bright future. "Maybe." It was a stretch, but "maybe" was as close to a promise as she was willing to offer.

"Okay." Kellie seemed satisfied with that. And relieved. "If you have to marry him, and he's going to be my new dad, I'll try my best to like him." She chewed on her bottom lip, and Josie could see the wheels in her mind clicking. And then the tentative query came. "Do you think he'll like me? Maybe just a little?"

Josie's chest tightened, and she found it hurt to breathe. How quick her daughter was to accept Seth! "What's not to like? You're beautiful, smart and sweeter than sugar." She lovingly ran her finger down the pert slope of Kellie's nose and made a silent vow that if Seth ever hurt her daughter by rejecting her, she'd make every day of his life a living hell.

Kellie laughed and spun around happily, arms spread wide. Her cascade of auburn spiral curls shimmered in the sunshine, and then she turned her lovely smile Josie's way. "So, when are you guys getting married?"

Josie wished she could drum up even half the enthusiasm her daughter possessed. "Probably Friday."

"Wow!" Bending down, she plucked a wildflower from a patch, then another, gathering a pretty yellow bouquet. "Can I be one of those girls who stands beside you and holds flowers?"

Josie managed a smile. "I'd love for you to be my maid of honor."

Kellie's eyes glowed with anticipation. "And will there be a big cake and a fancy dinner and dance afterward?"

Josie knew Kellie was remembering the wedding they'd attended last year for a friend of the family. It had been a lavish, traditional affair, with all the pomp and circumstance every young girl dreamed of. A beautiful white dress, a handsome groom who adored his bride, and vows that included loving and cherishing till death them did part.

Loving and cherishing wasn't part of the agreement. Just a quickie marriage that would ensure she kept the ranch in the family. "It's going to be a small, quiet ceremony," she said in answer to her daughter's question. "And there won't be a reception afterward."

Disappointment put a damper on Kellie's excitement. And then an idea revitalized the sparkle in her eyes. "Maybe I could bake you and Mr. O'Connor a wedding cake!"

Josie suppressed a groan at the thought of explaining a young girl's whimsy to Seth. "We'll see."

Crossing her arms over her chest and propping her backside on one of the fence's rungs, Josie watched her daughter frolic in the meadow, picking flowers and pretending to be a bride. It was obvious that Kellie didn't understand that she was marrying Seth because she *had* to and not because she wanted to. But Josie was okay with that because it eased her daughter's fears to believe her mother was willingly marrying Mr. O'Connor.

Seth, *her husband*. The idea was difficult to get used to, considering she'd long ago given up trying to find a man worthy of that title. She'd dated a few times over the years, but the men she'd gone out with had heard about her "reputation" and expected more from her than a dinner companion and friendly conversation. Fending off groping hands had become a frustrating and depressing process— so much so that she'd decided it was easier to forgo the rituals of dating.

As a result, though, her personal life was empty. Oh, she had Kellie to fill her days with smiles and laughter, but the long, lonely nights were the worst. Sometimes she'd remember how Seth's hands had felt on her body, the way he'd kissed her so eagerly, as if he couldn't get enough of her. In the dark of night, those memories were enough to make her ache with a need so acute she'd toss and turn restlessly until dawn.

But it wasn't just physical pleasure she wanted. She longed for love. She yearned to be cherished. Now, she was going to be some man's possession. Seth would be her husband, and the sensual privileges that came with that title made heat curl in her stomach.

She steeled herself against the pleasant sensation rippling through her veins. She refused to be Seth's plaything again, wouldn't let him use her body to slake his lust. She refused to allow him that intimacy and give him the power to break her heart again.

He'd be back in a few days to get her answer. She had no choice but to marry him if she wanted to keep the ranch; she knew and accepted that. But she had a stipulation of her own to add to their wedding deed—one that would benefit the both of them.

A marriage of convenience.

As promised, Seth came calling a few days later. At the break of dawn Wednesday morning, he rode up on his chestnut just as Mac and the other hands were heading out for the day. The six younger men on horseback abruptly stopped and watched Seth's approach, looking like a pack of vigilant brothers out to defend their sister's honor should the need arise.

They all knew Seth O'Connor would be their new boss and they didn't seem to be taking the change graciously. First thing Monday morning, she'd informed the men who worked for her about her upcoming nuptials, the circumstances surrounding the marriage, and reassured them it was nothing more than a business arrangement. She'd promised everyone that their jobs were secure as long as they wanted to stay and work on the Golden M.

She appreciated her men's concern and loyalty, but judging by the scowl on Seth's face, he didn't care for her overprotective ranch hands or the fact that they were treating him like an unwelcome guest.

Seth reined his mare to a stop a few yards away from her, his gaze warm and territorial as it touched upon her— as if he was staking a personal claim for the benefit of her men. She cursed the involuntary fluttering in her stomach, the instant surge of heat that sped through her veins. Resolutely, she told herself it was nothing more than nerves for the discussion ahead, and had absolutely *nothing* to do with the fact that there was still a deep, underlying awareness between them.

Josie thought she was prepared to confront him again and have the upper hand in the matter, but she hadn't anticipated him looking so good. Without a deep scowl on his face, Seth was an incredibly handsome man. No matter that she didn't like him, her faithless feminine senses noted and appreciated how virile and sexy he was—he so effortlessly epitomized what a *real* cowboy should look like. He was well built, his muscles honed, his latent strength evident in the easy way he handled his spirited mare and moved fluidly in the saddle. His lazy confidence came from years of working a ranch and being one with the animal beneath him.

He hadn't replaced the hat she now had in her possession, and his windblown hair gleamed in the early-morning sun creeping over the horizon. Curiously, there was none of the disdain in his blue eyes that had burned so brightly on Sunday. Instead, his gaze was very male and intensely direct. She found his brazen, sensual regard far more threatening than his anger.

She *hated* him, she chanted silently, keeping that reminder foremost in her mind.

Ignoring their avid audience, Seth urged his horse closer and leaned forward in the saddle. His mouth tipped in a beguiling smile just for her. "Hello, Josie."

"Seth." Folding her arms across her chest, she inclined her head and allowed a bland smile. "I'd say that it's nice to see you again, but we both know that would be a bald-faced lie."

His soft, intimate laughter reached out and caressed her. "Josie darlin', you sure do know how to flatter a man."

Her mouth pursed in irritation. It hadn't been her intention to flatter and seduce him, and the rogue knew it, too. He was twisting her words, deliberately being charming. The amicable act had to be for her men's benefit.

Mac sent the hands ahead and directed his gelding toward Josie and Seth.

"Want me to stick around, Josie girl?" Mac asked, his old weathered face creased with concern beneath the brim of his equally old leather hat.

"That won't be necessary." She didn't want any spectators for the "marriage of convenience" spiel she planned to give Seth. "Though since you're here, I'd like to introduce you to Seth formally."

While she made the introductions, both Seth and Mac moved their horses closer to each other until they were able to reach out and shake hands. Both of their grasps were firm, revealing none of the rivalry Josie had expected to flare between them. Amazingly, Seth's expression reflected a high regard for the older man.

"I'm looking forward to working with you," Seth said pleasantly. "And I'd appreciate it if you and the other hands would help me get familiarized with how the Golden M operates."

Josie gaped. *Oh, he was so smooth!*

Seth's easy, open personality earned Mac's respect and admiration. His eyes sparkled and his features were transformed by a personable smile. "We'll all try and make the transition as smooth as possible."

"I appreciate that," Seth said.

Traitor, Josie thought of her foreman.

As if hearing her private thoughts, Seth's gaze slid her way. *How 'bout you, Josie darlin'? You gonna make the transition easy on me?*

She smiled sweetly, but her gaze was filled with a not so demure answer. *Don't count on it.*

The devastatingly sinful grin curving his mouth turned

her knees to water. The message in his eyes was clear and caused her pulse to skip a beat. *Challenge accepted.*

Mac directed his prancing gelding around in the direction his men had gone. "Well, the two of you behave yourself."

The parting comment was as innocent as anything Mac had ever said to her, meant to keep her and Seth from fighting, she was sure. Unfortunately, the casual remark served to conjure up all kinds of misbehaving possibilities of the more sensual variety.

"I'll be back around noon to check in." With a tip of his hat, Mac was off, leaving a thin trail of dust in his wake.

"Looks like it's just you'n me," Seth said, his voice a low rumble of sound.

"And Kellie," she added, reminding him that he needed to keep her daughter's presence in mind. "Like Mac said, behave yourself."

"We'll see." Dismounting from his mare, he led her to the hitching post and tied off her reins, then returned to Josie. "You got a cup of coffee you can offer me?"

His presumptuousness annoyed her. All his easygoing civility was beginning to unnerve her and make her question what ulterior motives he might have up his sleeve. He was being way too nice and friendly.

Fine. She'd kill him with kindness, too. She was all for being cordial and making their arrangement as pleasant as possible for both of them. In exchange for a platonic marriage, she'd put up with a few of his idiosyncrasies.

She blew out a resigned breath. "I've got coffee and muffins up at the main house," she said, and before she changed her mind about being polite, she led the way.

CHAPTER FOUR

SETH followed Josie up to the house at a more leisurely pace, and came to the conclusion that the view from a few yards behind was more pleasurable than walking side by side. Her spine was unyielding, but she more than made up for that rigidity in the gentle sway of her hips and the way those long, graceful legs strode so determinedly toward the front porch.

He'd thought nothing could look sexier on Josie than those cutoffs she'd worn Sunday, but it seemed he was wrong. The full-length jeans she wore were old and faded but fitted her like a tailored glove. The soft, well-worn material hugged her small, toned bottom, molded to her slim thighs and gave his imagination something to consider for future fantasies.

Her blouse, tucked into the waistband of her jeans, was on the prim and proper side in comparison with her Sunday attire, as was the tight, single braid that fell halfway down her back. Her packaging appeared conservative, but what she didn't realize was that a man would have to be dead below the belt not to notice her lush curves.

He was far from immune in that department—his manhood was too quick to remind him that he was a twenty-nine-year-old male in his prime.

She cast a surreptitious glance over her shoulder to gauge his distance behind her, and he lifted his gaze from her jean-clad bottom and let a slow, shameless smile spread across his face. She looked momentarily startled, then quickly recovered.

"Is it necessary for you to lag behind?" she asked, her tone exasperated.

"No, not necessary at all," he drawled. "Just more en-joyable."

Her cheeks flushed, and she promptly turned back around and kept trudging toward the house, muttering something beneath her breath he couldn't decipher. It was probably for the best. He was certain whatever she had to say about him wasn't complimentary.

His good-natured attitude was throwing her off-kilter, which is precisely what he'd intended. He'd had three days of doing nothing except packing up his meager belongings and thinking about the various ways he could approach the wedding agreement with Josie. They'd be married, living in the same house and interacting on a daily basis for more years than he cared to think about. The only way they'd survive was if they agreed up front to leave the past where it belonged and make a pact to start out fresh.

It wouldn't be easy for either one of them, but it was a compromise he was willing to attempt in order to make life bearable.

Her leather work boots echoed off the steps as she gained the porch. At the front door she stopped and waited for him to catch up.

"Kellie is still sleeping," she said, her voice hushed. "I'd appreciate it if you kept your voice down when we go inside."

He lifted a dark brow, detecting a nervous energy about her that didn't sit well with him. "Is there going to be a need for me to raise it?"

"No." Quickly glancing away, she pulled open the screen door and entered the house.

He didn't believe her, but the only way he was going to find out what she was up to was follow her inside. They crossed through the living room to the kitchen, giving Seth a brief glimpse of the house he'd acquired. It seemed open and roomy, but then anything would appear large compared to the cramped cabin he'd been living in for the past couple of years. He was anxious to have a real bedroom again, to sleep on a comfortable mattress instead of the lumpy one he pulled out of the sofa bed every night.

The kitchen was decorated in soft pastels of peach and green, and the sweet fragrance of baked goods was enough to make his empty stomach grumble. An oak table sat in an adjoining kitchen nook, surrounded by six spindle back chairs. Pulling one out, he sat down and watched Josie retrieve two mugs from the cupboard and pour coffee into each. She sliced open what smelled like a still-warm apple spice muffin, slathered butter on the two ends and delivered one of the mugs of coffee and the fragrant bread to him.

He thanked her, but she seemed so preoccupied she only gave him an indistinct nod. She looked like she had something on her mind, and it was distracting her enough that she didn't realize she was waiting on him and being hospitable about it.

While she put cream and sugar in her coffee, he took a drink of his own. It was strong and black, just how he liked it. And the muffin was so light, fluffy and buttery it practically melted in his mouth. He was a man with a healthy appetite and he hated his own cooking. Marrying Josie was looking better with every bite of muffin.

He waited until she joined him at the table. She sat across from him, which wasn't surprising, considering how very businesslike she suddenly appeared. He almost expected her to take a piece of chalk, draw a dividing line between them and inform him that the side of the table he sat on was his, while the other was hers.

She didn't seem inclined to start the ball rolling on their conversation despite how anxious and edgy she looked, so he tossed out a question sure to start their discussion. "So, what'll it be, Josie? Marriage or eviction?"

Her green eyes filled with the first stirring of displeasure. "Neither one is a very attractive option."

He smiled and shrugged. "One is more gratifying than

the other,'' he said pointedly, though he knew she'd never consider the latter no matter how much she complained about the stipulation. ''It doesn't matter to me either way, but I'm eager to claim the Golden M and I'd like to know if I'll be taking on a wife and child.''

She took a sip of her coffee, then carefully set the mug back on the table, keeping her fingers wrapped around it. Then her gaze met his. ''I'd like to offer an alternative arrangement—''

''Marriage is part of the deal, Josie.'' Finished with his muffin, he pushed his plate aside. ''Your father stipulated it, and I'm not willing to jeopardize the deed to the Golden M by striking some other sort of bargain with you.''

''I understand that,'' she said indignantly. ''But I think I have a solution, one that would cater to both of us.''

He took a long drink of his coffee, studying her over the rim and wishing he knew what she intended. He'd find out soon enough, he supposed. ''I'm intrigued,'' he said, his tone a trifle mocking. ''By all means, let's hear your wonderful idea.''

Her chin lifted—showing that stubborn streak of hers. ''I want a marriage of convenience.''

He almost laughed out loud. *He'd just bet she would*! ''No.''

She frowned at him as if she couldn't believe he'd refuse such a golden opportunity. ''Seth, it's the best option available in our predicament. Our marriage could be like a partnership—''

''No.''

She blew out a frustrated breath. ''You're being unreasonable!'' Shoving back her chair, she stood and crossed the kitchen to the sink, where she dumped out the last of her coffee.

''*I'm* being unreasonable?'' He turned his chair around to look at her, incredulity replacing his earlier amusement.

"God, Josie, I'm not a monk, and I refuse to remain celibate for the next fifty years."

"Well…" Her eyes were wide, as though she was groping for a feasible reply. "You could see other women."

Anger vibrated through him. "That's not *my* style, Josie." She flinched at his pointed remark, but he didn't regret saying it. "I'm a one-woman man. I'd expect the same of you once we're married. Will that be a problem for you?"

She glared at him, something emotional shimmering in her gaze, an odd combination of hurt and deeply buried bitterness. "I'll be true to our wedding vows, but I have no desire to sleep with you."

His ego was beginning to feel a little bruised. "Be that as it may, you'll be my wife. Conjugal rights come with the package."

She huffed in annoyance. "If you'd give yourself time to consider the idea, you'd see that a marriage of convenience would work perfectly between us."

"*No.*" The one word boomed like thunder in the kitchen. So much for keeping his voice down in consideration of her sleeping daughter. "You're not in a position to negotiate, Josie. We'll sleep in the same bed, and if you don't like that arrangement, then you don't have to marry me. That's your *only* choice."

She opened her mouth to reply, then immediately snapped it shut again. "Why are you making this so difficult?" She started toward him, waving a hand in the air in aggravation. "We can't stand each other, so why would you want your *rights*?"

"Because *forever* is a mighty long time, and I've got a fairly healthy sex drive," he said bluntly. And despite every reason he had to hate her, he was still strongly attracted to her. "Just because we don't like one another doesn't mean we can't enjoy the more physical aspects of marriage. So, what will it be, Josie?"

She stood by the kitchen-nook window, her back to him, staring out at the expanse of yard separating the main barn from the house. She was silent for so long, he began to wonder if she'd seriously consider giving him the ranch because she couldn't stand the thought of his touching her.

"Fine," she said flatly after long moments had passed, keeping her back to him. "A real marriage it will be."

Damned if he didn't experience a rush of relief at her answer. He didn't question it, but the hum of anticipation of being with her was already pulsing through his blood. "Good. Then I'll expect your cooperation starting on our wedding night."

She whirled around so fast her braid flew over her shoulder and slapped her chest. "You can't be serious."

He just looked at her, which was all the answer she needed. She wanted to postpone the inevitable as long as possible, and he wasn't going to budge on his decision.

Panic etched her expression. "I need time to get used to the idea of...of..."

"Making love with me?" he offered.

"Yes!"

"What's there to get used to?" Stretching his legs out in front of him, he folded his hands over his belly. His gaze locked on hers, and he let a wicked smile lift his mouth. "It's not as though we're strangers. We were good together, Josie, remember? You used to like the way I touched you, the way I made you come apart for me and beg for more."

Her face inflamed. Jamming her hands on her hips, she leaned toward him, close enough that he could see the angry hurt flaring to life in her eyes. "That was before I learned what a rat you were and that you were just using me!"

He laughed at that. "That's like the pot calling the kettle black, don't you think?"

She stood there, her hands balled into fists. And then, as

if she realized she was fighting a losing battle, the fire went out of her and the tension in her body eased. "Fine, Seth," she said. "I'll agree to your terms, but just know up front that I'm not going to be a willing participant."

He controlled his rising fury with supreme effort. It wasn't as though he was an ugly troll! "Oh, I think you will be."

She touched her tongue to her bottom lip, where a triumphant smile lingered. "A woman has more control over such things than a man does, so don't count on it, O'Connor."

She started to turn away to end the discussion, but he wasn't about to let her have the last word, not when he was so damned furious he wanted to...kiss her and make her burn for him, until that haughty control of hers incinerated beneath the onslaught of his mouth and hands.

Fast as a whip, he grabbed her wrist and pulled her toward where he sat. She stumbled backward at the unexpected move, a gasp of shock catching in her throat. Another tug, and she was sprawled inelegantly across his lap, her bottom pressing against his hard thighs. She lost the use of one arm because it was wedged between her side and his chest, and he still had her other hand manacled.

She was trapped, and she knew it, too.

The hand supporting her back found the end of her braid, and he slowly wound the long, thick plait around his fist, forcing her head back and her lips to part on a gasp. His eyes must have been glittering with his barely suppressed rage because alarm etched her features.

"Seth..." Her voice was shaky, the pulse at the base of her throat fluttering wildly like a trapped butterfly. It matched the throbbing beneath the press of his thumb on the pulse point in her wrist.

He almost let her go, almost gave in to her soft plea, but as he stared at that ripe mouth of hers and thought of how good she'd taste, the slow heat of desire settled low in his belly and urged him on.

"I'm more than counting on your being a willing participant in our bed, darlin'," he murmured, his tone low and deep and husky. "In fact, I'd be more than happy to prove here and now just how willing you'll be."

She tried to turn away as his lips descended, but the hand wrapped around her braid restrained her. His mouth covered hers and she stiffened, clamping her lips tightly shut to keep him out. Undeterred, he tried a different approach. He flicked his tongue along the seam, then nibbled on her bottom lip before suckling the lush fullness into his mouth.

A groan rumbled in her throat, but her jaw remained unyielding, despite his efforts to gain entry. He found himself smiling at how stubborn she could be, and what had started as a punishment became a contest of wills Seth was determined to win.

Since he was having little luck with her mouth, he seduced her with slow, damp kisses to her throat, letting his tongue lap the skin of her neck, his teeth grazing along her jaw until she trembled. He took his time, leisurely stripping away her resistance until she was overwhelmed with the sensual sensations he was creating.

Gradually, she stopped struggling. Her chest heaved with panting breaths, and the hand he'd manacled with his fingers grew slack. He went back to her mouth for another try; this time she was waiting for him, her lips already parted. She didn't resist him when he settled his mouth over hers, didn't protest when his tongue sought entrance and glided silkily along hers.

Hunger and need ripped through him, taking him by surprise. He'd meant to teach her a lesson...not fall into a trap of his own making!

Letting go of her hand, he gently framed her face between his palms and opened his mouth wider over hers. His tongue swept deeply, swirling sensually. Her response was tentative at first, then she moaned in acquiescence and gave him exactly what he was after. Surrender and pleasure.

Kissing her was just as magical as he remembered. Her mouth was just as honeyed sweet and generous as in his dreams. No one had ever matched him so perfectly; no one had ever excited him more than the woman now sitting in his lap. His body hardened, and he thought about how good it would feel to bury himself in her sleek warmth, how incredible she'd feel moving beneath him, her legs wrapped around his hips.

Their wedding night suddenly seemed a million years away, and he wondered if he could talk her into getting married that afternoon.

Something gouged his shoulders, and it took him a moment to realize that Josie was using the heel of her palms to push him away, to try to break free. She was no longer caught up in that enchanting spell—she must have finally realized just how willing and eager she'd been.

Satisfied that he'd proved his point, he lifted his lips from hers, removed his hands from her face and let her go. She shoved hard at that moment and squirmed away…and slid off his thighs and dropped like a rock onto the hardwood floor.

She winced and moaned at the excruciating impact, then glared up at him as if it was all his fault. Her fire was back, seething in her eyes. He wondered if she was angry at him for kissing her or angrier at herself for kissing him back and liking every minute of it.

He grinned down at her. "So much for a woman having more control than a man does, hmm?" he couldn't resist teasing. His gibe earned him a scathing look, but he didn't care because he was having too much fun. "Since you seemed to enjoy that kiss every bit as much as I did, a marriage of convenience is out of the question."

"Go to hell," she snapped.

He chuckled deeply. "You just put me there, darlin',"

he said, referring to his physical condition. "But we'll take care of the problem on our wedding night."

Before she had a chance to respond—and he had a feeling her reply would have had a heated, insulting edge to it—Seth heard a heavy *thump, thump, thump* coming from the other room and watched as Josie scrambled up from the floor. She straightened just as her daughter shuffled into the kitchen, looking from her disheveled mother to Seth.

The young girl's green eyes widened with wariness at finding him in the kitchen. Instinctively, she moved closer to Josie, seeking reassurance. Josie placed an arm around Kellie's shoulders in a protective manner, and his jaw tensed in annoyance. Did she think he was some kind of monster who would hurt her child?

"Morning, honey," she greeted the girl, her tone amazingly even and pleasant considering that only moments before she'd been seething with anger and indignation.

Seth found the sweet, charming Josie a fascinating contrast to the spitfire who'd been draped across his lap, that sassy mouth of hers kissing him with a wild passion that matched his own. The woman was an exciting blend of contradictions, and he experienced an inexplicable rush of male challenge at the thought of discovering all those layers of contrasts—in bed, and out.

"Morning, Mom," Kellie responded automatically, still staring at Seth.

Very gently, Josie tipped the girl's chin up so Kellie had no choice but to transfer her gaze from Seth to her mother. It seemed Josie wanted her daughter's complete attention. "Remember we discussed Mr. O'Connor and how he'll be living here?"

Kellie nodded. "Yeah, you said he's going to be my new dad."

He watched Josie visibly draw in a steady breath, as if she wanted to refute the fact but couldn't. "That's right. He'll be your *step*dad, by marriage." Taking her daughter's hand, she drew her closer to Seth and made the more formal introductions. "Kellie, I'd like you to meet Mr. O'Connor."

Kellie politely extended her hand toward him, an automatic gesture dictated by the good manners she'd obviously been taught. "It's nice to meet you, Mr. O'Connor," she said softly and with more reserve than her mother possessed.

He thought about standing but changed his mind, not wanting to risk intimidating her with his size. This way, they were at eye level and on an equal footing. Gently, he folded her small hand in between his two much larger ones, which made her take another step closer. At any time she could have pulled back her arm and he would have let her sever the contact between them. She didn't so much as tug or try to wriggle her fingers loose. Her head tilted slightly, and her expression reflected a childlike fascination and curiosity.

A shy smile lifted her lips, and he was a goner.

The simple trust they established in that moment expanded Seth's chest with a peculiar emotion he was hard-pressed to name. It warmed him and settled somewhere near his heart. Suddenly, "Mr. O'Connor" seemed much too proper and unapproachable.

"It's very nice to meet you, too, Kellie," he said, giving her his best winning smile. Unabashed pleasure lit up the young girl's eyes, and he was again aware of that warm, fuzzy feeling spreading inside him. "And since your mother and I will be married, you can call me—"

"Mr. O'Connor," Josie interjected firmly.

Seth glanced Josie's way and lifted a dark brow in silent question, but she didn't relent or soften. She stubbornly held her ground, her cool gaze making it clear she didn't want him establishing any close attachment with her daughter.

He understood her protectiveness, he honestly did. She

didn't want their agreement and the dissension between them to affect her daughter on an emotional level, and it was that deep, instinctive perception that made him patient with Josie and her zealous maternal behavior. He supposed if this sweet, guileless girl was his own, he'd be heedful of anyone trying to gain her trust, as well. But considering the years ahead of them, he wanted an amicable, open relationship with the girl who would be his stepdaughter. The girl he'd be responsible for. Surely Josie would want that, too?

Ignoring Josie and her withering glare, he shifted his gaze back to Kellie, who appeared a little uneasy because of the obvious tension swirling between the two adults.

Patting her hand one last time before letting go, he said simply, "How about you just call me Seth for now?"

"Okay...Seth." She ducked her head to cover up a modest smile, but not before he caught the hopeful glimmer in her pretty eyes, giving Seth the distinct impression the girl wanted his acceptance. Odd, considering her mother's adverse feelings toward him.

Josie placed her hands on her daughter's shoulders and directed her to sit on the other side of the table. "Mr. O'Connor...Seth and I were just finishing up our conversation." Her tone was as brisk as her movements as she crossed to the refrigerator and pulled out a carton of eggs, a slab of ham and a tub of butter. "I'm sure he's anxious to be on his way, and I need to fix you breakfast before I get to work." Setting the items by the stove, she shot Seth a pointed look. "Don't you have things you need to tend to at Paradise Wild?"

"Nope," he drawled lazily, refusing to take her subtle hint to leave. Standing, he picked up his empty mug and took it to the counter, where he helped himself to a fresh cup of coffee. "Actually, I don't have a darn thing to do for the next two days. I quit Paradise Wild and have all the time in the world until we get married."

She cracked an egg on the edge of a glass bowl with more force than necessary, not looking happy about that fact. Especially since he didn't seem inclined to spend his idle time elsewhere.

"Then maybe you can stay and have breakfast with us," came the tentative request from the kitchen nook.

Seth and Josie turned their heads to glance at Kellie in one simultaneous motion. Seth grinned at the thoughtful invitation; Josie frowned at what she obviously construed as a horrible suggestion.

"Why, thank you, Kellie. That's an offer I find difficult to refuse," Seth said before Josie pounced on the opportunity to make up an excuse for him to be on his way. Kellie beamed at his compliment, pleased with her idea. "Good food, the company of two beautiful, sweet women. What more could a man ask for?"

Turning on the back burner of the stove, Josie placed a skillet on top of the flames. "Not to get food poisoning?" she offered, giving him a sugary smile.

He dipped his head and chuckled close to her ear. "Getting sick wouldn't be such a bad thing, not with you as my wife. I kinda like the thought of you being my nursemaid."

She picked up a sharp knife and sliced the ham, her movements quick and efficient. "And I kinda like the thought of you being at my mercy."

He winced as he watched her wield that knife with so much skill. "Touché," he murmured, and moved back to the table and more friendly conversation with Kellie.

Josie watched him go, resenting the way he was insinuating himself into their lives so easily and swaying her impressionable young daughter with little effort. She couldn't very well tell him to go buy his breakfast at the nearest diner without Kellie thinking she was a witch, so here she was, preparing scrambled eggs, ham and muffins for a man she didn't like, a man who'd dared to kiss her and take liberties she'd allowed no other man for the past eleven years.

A man who'd openly gloated at her response. A man who wanted to claim his conjugal rights on their wedding night.

The thought of making love with Seth was enough to send a frisson of panic through her, as well as another emotion she didn't want to analyze. If she couldn't fend off a simple kiss, how was she going to immunize herself against the feel of his hands sliding over her body, touching her in places that quivered to life when he dared to look at her with that smoldering heat in his eyes?

Frustrated with the direction of her thoughts, she took her aggravation out on the eggs in the bowl, beating them until they were frothy, while the slices of ham sizzled in the skillet. Two more days until her wedding night. Two more days to figure out how to handle the situation.

"So, do you ride much, Kellie?" Josie heard Seth ask her daughter. Eavesdropping provided her with the perfect excuse not to think about her upcoming nuptials...or her physical surrender to Seth O'Connor.

"Yeah," Kellie said in her quiet voice. "I have my own horse, Juliette, and I try to ride her every day."

Seth smiled at Kellie, all charm and persuasion. "Maybe you and I could go for a ride together sometime. You could show me some of your favorite spots on the Golden M."

"There's a place I like over in the west pasture. There's a creek and a big tree." Excitement tinged her words.

He took a sip of his coffee. "Sounds great. I'd like to go see it."

"Okay." Kellie glanced up at him from beneath half-lowered lashes, bashful but curious. "Do you, um, have any kids?"

Josie's stomach dropped to her knees, and she almost lost the grip she had on the skillet of fried ham and scrambled eggs she was transferring to a platter on the counter.

Dear Lord, how could such an innocent question cause so much inner turmoil?

Watching Seth's expression carefully and seeing nothing more than a growing affection for her own daughter that she knew she was helpless to discourage, she retrieved plates and silverware and carried them to the table.

"No, I don't have any kids," he told Kellie. "But I've got a niece and nephew. Brianna is six and Brendan is four. They're my brother's kids and they'll be your cousins once your mom and I are married."

Brightening at the prospect of having an extended family, Kellie leaned forward in her seat. "Will I get to meet them?"

Seth hesitated long enough to cause Josie concern. Knowing how vehemently Jay had hated the McAllisters, she wondered if Jay's hostility toward her family had ebbed over the years or still remained as bitter as it had been when she'd been a teenager. She'd spent eleven years deftly avoiding anything to do with the O'Connor name, and though she and Seth were forced to forge a truce because of her father, she realized she had no idea how this latest turn of events would affect Seth's brother.

The way Seth was apparently thinking up a tactful response was a good indication that Jay hadn't miraculously buried the hatchet. And if that was the case, she refused to subject her daughter to the same cruelty she'd endured as a child and intended to inform Seth as much.

Seth offered Kellie a noncommittal reply. "Eventually, yes, you'll meet your cousins."

"Will they be at the wedding?" she asked hopefully.

"No, they won't be," Josie cut in, setting the platter of eggs and ham in the center of the table, along with a plate of muffins. She sat at the end, between Seth and Kellie. "It'll be just you, me and Seth on Friday. The ceremony will be short and simple." She looked to Seth for confirmation.

A wry smile touched his generous mouth. "Short and simple," he echoed.

They ate breakfast, and Josie watched as Seth and Kellie developed an easy friendship. Begrudgingly, she had to admit that Seth was wonderful with her daughter. No matter how much she and Seth disliked one another, that animosity hadn't transferred to Kellie. She was at least grateful for that, while at the same time she worried about Kellie becoming too attached to Seth, a man who only had one agenda on his mind: claiming the Golden M.

Once breakfast was over and Kellie had cleared the dishes from the table, Josie sent her daughter up to her room to change, then start on her outdoor chores. Automatically, she refilled Seth's coffee cup, berating herself for softening a little at the appreciation in his gaze and the husky way he said thank-you.

She filled the sink with soapy water. Dipping her hands into the suds, she scrubbed the platter, then finally asked the question that had preyed on her mind for the past half hour. "So, was Jay happy to learn you now own the Golden M?"

"He was ecstatic that the property is back in the family," Seth replied, his deep voice laced with a bitter edge. "But he's not too happy that I won't share it."

She glanced over her shoulder, meeting his gaze. "It would seem logical, you two joining the property again."

"It's not even a remote possibility, Josie."

She was relieved to hear that. Even though marriage to Seth would secure her half of the Golden M, she didn't want to fight with him over the fate of her family's ranch. And she certainly didn't want it to become O'Connor property again.

She heard the front door close and a moment later watched as her daughter skipped down to the barn to tend to her chores. Kellie looked so young and carefree...and happy. It made Josie's heart twist peculiarly, because she had a feeling Kellie's exhilaration was linked to Seth…the man who would become her dad.

She wished she could be as excited about Seth becoming her husband, but whenever she thought about her upcoming nuptials, dread was foremost in her mind. This was a man who'd used her and hurt her, who obviously had no qualms about using her once again to gain what he wanted. That fact stung most of all.

She rinsed off the skillet and set it on the dish rack to dry, her mind drifting back to Seth's brother. "How does Jay feel about our marriage?"

Scooting out his chair, Seth grabbed his coffee cup and brought it to her to wash. She took the mug from his hand, careful not to touch him. Her nerves couldn't take much more physical contact with him.

Leaning a hip against the counter, he crossed his arms over his wide chest, looking way too masculine. He smelled of leather and something inherently male. "Let's just say that he's not quite ready to welcome you into the fold, but I'm confident he'll come around in time."

Done with the dishes, she unplugged the drain and rinsed her hands, remembering still how cruel Jay had been to her when she was growing up, all for something she'd had no control over.

"I don't want Kellie around that kind of animosity," she said, facing Seth. "I won't allow Jay to take his grudges out on her."

His dark brows snapped together. "And you think I'd subject her to that?"

No, something inside told her he'd never be so heartless, but she couldn't find the words to apologize for insulting him. "She's my daughter, Seth. You can't blame me for wanting to protect her from any kind of unpleasantness between our families."

"I always take care of what's mine, Josie." His voice

held an odd tightness, despite his casual tone. "Jay won't be a problem."

And she and Kellie would be his, bound by marriage. Her pulse picked up at the thought. She'd never relied on a man to fight her battles before, or to take care of her. She'd always tackled any problems on her own. It was odd to think that Seth would be the one who handled any trouble that arose—including dealing with his brother.

She blew out a taut breath. Not wanting to discuss any more personal issues or think of Seth as her husband and protector, she made a production of checking the watch on her wrist, then gave him a dismissive smile. "Unlike you, I don't have the luxury of frittering the day away. I've got work to do, Seth."

"I can take a hint," he said, and straightened. "I have some things I need to attend to in town anyway. While I'm there, I'll make our appointment with Reverend Wilcox for Friday at one. I'll pick you and Kellie up at noon." He moved away from her but paused in the doorway leading to the living room to glance back at her. His dark eyes glinted with wicked humor, and his mouth curved in an outrageously rakish grin. "And feel free to get yourself something sexy to wear for our wedding night."

A flash of heat jolted down her spine and settled in all her intimate places. "Don't count on it, O'Connor," she muttered grimly.

His responding chuckle was deep, rich and confident. "I love a good challenge, Josie, especially if it's anything like this morning's." He winked audaciously, then walked away.

Her face flushed at his blatant reminder of her acquiescence, the way she'd let him kiss her so sensually, and especially the way she'd responded with so much abandon.

Armed with the knowledge of his seduction tactics, next time she wouldn't be so easily cajoled by his slow, coaxing kisses and insidious caresses. She'd agreed to give him her body and had no choice but to submit physically to the man who would be her husband, but she was fiercely determined not to let him touch her emotionally as he had earlier.

If Seth loved a good challenge, she'd give him one.

Packed with feminine wiles, a resolute smile curved her mouth. "You have no idea what you're up against, Mr. O'Connor."

CHAPTER FIVE

THE bride wore black, from the sprigs of dyed baby's breath arranged in her upswept hair to the tips of her black high-heeled shoes. The groom sported denim, chambray, a casual tweed jacket and a new tan Stetson. The young maid of honor had opted for a more cheerful splash of pink chiffon and an enthusiastic smile that reached her sparkling green eyes.

They made quite a trio of contrasting moods, ranging from dismal acceptance, to resigned satisfaction, to guileless excitement. The variety of emotions shimmering between them was enough to make Reverend Wilcox shift uncomfortably and clear his throat repeatedly before opening his Bible and beginning the traditional marriage ceremony.

Seth listened to the minister perform the simple wedding service, his gaze riveted to the woman standing stiffly beside him. Her hands were clasped tightly in front of her, and she held her head high and proud, despite what she obviously deemed the worst of circumstances—a life sentence shackling her to a man she abhorred.

A humorous grin tugged the corner of his mouth, but he didn't dare let it develop. Her somber expression, combined with her stark attire and rigid posture, gave the impression of a woman in mourning. He didn't doubt that her choice of dark apparel had been calculated, worn as a deliberate insult to the marriage she'd been forced into.

What Josie failed to realize, though, was that black was an extremely complimentary color on her. It enhanced her smooth, creamy complexion, made her green eyes gleam like polished emeralds and brought out fiery, burnished

69

highlights in the curly auburn hair she'd piled atop her head.

The cut of her black dress was simple and plain, but there was nothing casual about the way the clingy material outlined the fullness of her breasts and draped elegantly over her slim hips to just above the knee. Smoke-hued stockings only served to entice a man's eye to her slender, graceful legs.

His gaze flickered past his reluctant bride to the young, pretty girl standing beside Josie, who seemed completely enthralled by the reverend's wedding speech. She was clutching a handpicked bouquet of flowers bound with a pink ribbon that matched the one she'd tied in her hair to keep her waist-length spiral curls away from her face. Her pale pink dress suited her youth and innocence, and heightened the happily-ever-after yearning Seth saw shining in her eyes.

Kellie glanced his way, saw him watching her and smiled impishly. In that instant, Seth wanted to give the girl her fairy-tale ending. It was an odd sensation, one he didn't want to contemplate too deeply, especially since he didn't have the power to grant that particular wish. Not without Josie's cooperation. Finding that last thought disturbing—that gaining Josie's cooperation was beginning to matter to him—he shifted his attention back to the man in front of them.

With his customary wedding speech over, Reverend Wilcox glanced at Seth expectantly. "Do you have a ring for your bride?"

Buying Josie a wedding band hadn't crossed his mind, and he felt somewhat chagrined at his blunder. "No, I don't."

The older man's frown reflected his disapproval of Seth's lack of consideration for the woman who would become his wife. "Then why don't you just hold Josie's left hand while you recite your vows?" he suggested.

Turning toward Josie, Seth clasped her cool hand in his warm one and noticed that her small slender fingers trembled ever so slightly against his palm—the only outward sign that she was nervous. Taking a deep breath and staring straight into her eyes, he repeated the minister's words, promising a lifetime commitment to her in a strong, steady voice. When it came her turn to agree to love, honor and cherish him, her mouth said, "I do," but her eyes conveyed a more defiant message: *I won't.*

Seth wasn't the least bit surprised by her stubbornness. He had weeks, months, even years, to break through that resistance of hers. It was a suddenly sobering thought.

"I now pronounce you man and wife," Reverend Wilcox stated, closing his Bible and glancing at the newly married couple. "You may, ahhh...kiss your bride." His uncertainty over the situation was apparent in the way he stumbled over the final part of the service.

The kiss loomed in front of them. Josie took a visible step back, establishing her own boundaries and silently proclaiming that she had no desire to engage in such a public display of affection. Their circumstances were anything but ideal or romantic, but judging by Kellie's delighted expression, she fully expected them to partake in the traditional sealing of wedding vows.

Not wanting to disappoint the young girl or pass up the chance to rattle his new bride's prim composure, he tipped his Stetson back and lowered his head toward Josie's. Her gaze widened, evidence of her surprise at his boldness. Just as his mouth would have touched hers, she turned her head so his lips skimmed her soft cheek.

He chuckled deeply; he couldn't help himself. It was so like Josie to best him at the last moment that he should have anticipated her move. He straightened, then noticed that she looked entirely too pleased with herself for evading his more intimate kiss.

He leaned closer, so his mouth was near her ear. "I'll

collect plenty of kisses tonight to make up for that one loss,'' he promised in a husky murmur.

Her face turned a warm, flustered shade of pink, and fire flashed in her eyes. Mindful of their audience, she didn't issue a sassy retort the way he knew she would have if they'd been alone.

Reverend Wilcox smiled, the gesture full of relief that his part was done. ''Congratulations to the both of you.''

Seth reached out and shook the minister's hand. ''Thank you.''

Kellie wrapped her arms around Josie and hugged her tightly. ''Wow, you're really married!'' she exclaimed happily.

Josie returned Kellie's embrace. ''Imagine that,'' she quipped, her voice lacking her daughter's excitement. She glanced at Seth, her businesslike gaze meeting his over Kellie's head. ''Ready to head home?''

Home. His chest swelled with indescribable emotions. He'd fulfilled his end of the bargain he'd struck with Jake McAllister. He'd married Josie, promised to take care of her and her daughter and gained the Golden M. It was heady to realize he now had a place to call his own, but he suspected the battle with Josie was just beginning.

Seth thanked Reverend Wilcox for performing the ceremony on such short notice, then the three of them headed down the aisle to the front of the small chapel with Kellie skipping ahead. Seth brazenly touched his hand to Josie's spine, his fingers caressing that sensitive spot through the thin material of her dress. Her breath caught, and she attempted to move out of his reach, but he lightly grasped her elbow, keeping her by his side.

She glared up at him, and he bestowed her with a charming grin. He stroked his thumb along the silky-soft skin under her arm—slow, sensuous circles that made the pulse at the base of her throat flutter despite her attempts to remain aloof. And then there was the telltale way the tips of her lovely breasts tightened and strained against the front of her dress.

It was a start.

"I'm a man who likes plenty of physical contact, Josie darlin'," he drawled, his tone low and intimate. "As my bride, you might as well get used to me touching you."

Casting him a sideways glance, she batted her lashes at him. "Why, Seth, that's like asking me to get used to the touch of a snake." The smile curving her mouth managed to combine innocence and a more insulting element. "I despise snakes."

His deep laughter followed them out of the chapel. "We'll see about that, bride."

Determined to treat her marriage as nothing more than a business deal, Josie headed up to her room to change into jeans and a blouse as soon as they arrived back home. She planned to spend the rest of the afternoon in the office down in the stable so she wouldn't have to be around Seth.

Just as she was struggling with the zipper at the back of her dress, her bedroom door opened. She spun around, her breath catching sharply when Seth strolled in, as bold as you please.

His audacity irritated her. "What do you think you're doing?"

A slow grin lifted his mouth. "Don't worry, Josie, it's too early yet to request my conjugal rights." His gaze flickered the length of her, making her traitorous body tingle from head to toe. "Though that would be an enjoyable way to pass the afternoon...."

The thought of heated bodies and tangled sheets flitted through her mind, and her heart tripled its beat. "Forget it."

He chuckled, then advanced toward where she was standing by the large four-poster bed, his steps slow and predatory. "I suppose I can wait until tonight. That'll give you all afternoon to anticipate what's to come." He trailed a finger along her cheek and across her bottom lip, bringing nerve endings to life with that tender touch.

Her stomach tumbled, and she summoned the willpower to push his hand away before she succumbed to his shameless seduction. "More like time to dread our wedding night."

"Ouch." He feigned a wince. "You sure know how to damage a man's ego."

Not in the mood for his sensual sparring, she moved away from him. The whirlwind events of the past week had her strung tight emotionally. "What do you want, Seth?"

"Just thought I'd unpack my belongings." He dropped the duffel and garment bags he held in one hand onto her bed, then shrugged out of the tweed jacket he'd donned for their wedding. "Did you make room for my things?"

She rubbed the slow throbbing beginning in her temple. "No." She'd agreed to allow him his conjugal rights, but she hadn't made any concessions regarding his occupying the same bedroom. This was her sanctuary, a place for her to escape and be alone, and she didn't want to share it. Especially with him. She pasted on a smile. "I don't suppose you'd consider sleeping in the guest room and keeping your personal things there?"

Irritation sparked in his deep blue eyes. "We're married, Josie. Husband and wife." Digging into his duffel, he withdrew a plain blue cotton T-shirt and began unbuttoning the crisp chambray one. "I'm not about to sneak into your bed every night, then leave before dawn to go to a separate room."

Every night. It sounded as though Seth *did* have a healthy sexual appetite. She swallowed thickly at the thought of enduring endless nights of Seth's slow, silky kisses, his warm caresses, his body possessing hers, and knew maintaining control of her emotions would be vital to protect more vulnerable territory—like her heart.

Disgruntled that he insisted on invading the only personal space she had, but knowing her arguments wouldn't sway him, she moved to the closet and pushed her clothes over to make room for his things. Once she'd given him ample space there, she began clearing out the top two dresser drawers for him to use.

She heard him changing into his T-shirt, then unbuckle his belt to tuck the bottom into the waistband of his jeans. She gave him enough time to complete the task—she wasn't ready for the intimacy of watching him change. When she finally turned around, she caught him admiring the black Stetson she'd blasted a hole into less than a week ago. It sat proudly displayed on her bedpost like a prized souvenir.

He glanced over his shoulder, humor dancing in his eyes. With a flick of his finger, he spun the hat around on the post. "Hmm, nice trophy, Josie."

"You think so?" She tilted her head, regarding the Stetson appreciatively before transferring her gaze to the new tan one he'd put back on his head. "I'm considering starting a collection of them."

His smile widened into a disarmingly flirtatious grin. "This one you'll have to earn." He caressed the brim with a finger and winked at her. "Be good tonight and I might let you put it on your bedpost."

Infuriated to feel her cheeks glow warmly at his sexually meaningful comment, she reached deep for a disparaging retort. "I much prefer the thrill of shooting it off your head."

The rogue laughed, not insulted in the least.

Feeling as though the situation was slipping out of her control—how could she battle with someone when he refused to rise to the bait?—she grabbed a pair of jeans and a blouse and stormed into the adjoining bathroom to change.

She didn't exit until she heard Seth leave the bedroom.

*   *   *

The countdown to their wedding night had begun.

Josie tried concentrating on paperwork for the Golden M but found she couldn't keep her gaze off the clock on the wall in her office. Every time she glanced up, which was entirely too often, it seemed some invisible finger had bumped up the minute hand half an hour. She'd been sitting behind her desk for almost three hours now, yet had accomplished nothing but brooding and worrying.

Groaning irritably, she tossed the feed bill onto her desk and gave up on her attempt to keep her mind occupied and off Seth. It was no use—the man who'd become her husband, as well as the quickly approaching night, totally consumed her thoughts until she wanted to scream just to release the tension building within her.

It was difficult to believe how her life had changed, and so suddenly and drastically. In a span of less than a week, she'd lost her father and had no idea where he was or if he'd return, forfeited half of the Golden M and now belonged to a man she had every reason to hate. A man who didn't seem the least bit discouraged by her aloofness but accepted her cool regard as a challenge instead.

Feeling restless, she stood and went to the only window in the office, which faced the east pasture and the numerous pens that covered a few acres of land. She saw Seth and Mac standing at one of the fences bordering the corral Seth had put his mare into that afternoon. The two were talking amicably; no doubt Seth was taking advantage of her foreman's knowledge and familiarizing himself with the operation of the ranch.

Seth laughed at something Mac said, and her pulse quickened as the unguarded moment transformed Seth's features, making him look incredibly young, handsome and kind. Like the boy she'd known in high school before she'd learned his interest in her was all a sham. Her heart twisted at the bittersweet memories, and she swallowed to ease the huge ache in her chest.

Seth gave the older man a companionable slap on the back, then headed toward the stables. By the time he walked into the office, she was sitting behind her desk, pretending interest in the invoice she hadn't been able to focus her attention on earlier.

Glancing up, she shot him a piqued look. "Don't you know how to knock?"

He lifted a dark brow and continued into the office, his masculine presence dominating the small room. "Is there a reason why I need to?"

"I'm busy and I'd rather not be disturbed." Her prim tone did nothing to discourage his progress toward her.

Wicked amusement played across his features. "Can't be all that busy considering I saw you standing at the window a moment ago."

She scowled, unable to come up with a fitting explanation or caustic response to his observation. He propped his hip on the edge of her desk, sitting so close his leg brushed her thigh. Awareness rippled through her, but he appeared unaffected by their close proximity. As subtly as possible, she shifted away so he was no longer touching her and sending her senses into a tailspin.

He tipped his hat back on his head. "You ready to call it a day, bride?"

Frowning at him, she set the feed bill on a pile of invoices on her desk. "Don't call me that."

"Why not? You're my bride until we consummate our marriage." His voice was low and filled with husky nuances. "After tonight you'll be my wife."

"Don't be so presumptuous about tonight, O'Connor," she said, challenging his arrogant statement.

"Making you my wife is not an assumption, but a fact, *Mrs. O'Connor*," he replied with too much confidence. "Tomorrow morning, you'll wake up a brand-new woman."

She choked on incredulous laughter. "You think you're that good, do you?"

He leaned closer and murmured seductively, "You of all people should know I am. You might have used me eleven years ago for your own purposes, but I believe the pleasure was mutual."

Her breath hitched in her throat at his crass reminder of how gullible she'd been back then, how easily he'd seduced her until she let him do things to her that still had the ability to make her blush. She'd found his caresses thrilling, could still remember how that tight coil of need he built within her unraveled upon the first deep stroke of his body into hers. The pleasure he'd given her had been so intense she'd nearly splintered into a thousand pieces. He'd always been right there with her at that crucial moment, burying his face in the crook of her neck and moaning her name as his entire body shuddered over hers.

She'd given him everything, and he'd taken her heart, her love, and ruthlessly crushed her hopes and dreams, leaving her entire world shattered. Now, she wanted to inflict on him some of the pain she'd lived with for eleven years.

"You overestimate yourself, Seth," she said, her tone flat and cold. "It was all an act."

He stared at her, a muscle in his jaw ticking. His eyes glittered with dark emotions, and he suddenly looked like the same dangerous outlaw who'd come to claim her only days before. Josie experienced a prickle of unease. Oh, Lord, had she finally pushed him too far?

After what seemed like an eternity, he released a long, harsh breath rife with frustration and slid from her desk. Moving to the window, he braced a forearm along the frame and stared outside. His back was rigid, his lean posture unyielding.

She'd hurt him. The knowledge wasn't as gratifying as she would have thought.

Josie squeezed her eyes shut, hating the regret rippling through her and the apology hovering on her lips. What did she have to be sorry for? Seth had certainly had his own agenda eleven years ago and gotten exactly what he'd wanted. Revenge on a McAllister. And she'd lived with the pain of the rumors that had circulated about her and the stigma of being considered "easy". And for the first few years after Kellie's birth, she'd had to endure the unkind whispers of her daughter's parentage.

Seth turned around, shadows of old pain lining his features, though his gaze was purposeful. "You know, Josie, I understand our situation isn't ideal, but I'm willing to compromise and make things work between us. Why do you insist on baiting me?" When she didn't offer an answer, he added, "Why can't you at least meet me halfway?"

The soft plea in his voice wove through her, reaching places she didn't want him to touch. A part of her wanted to put their differences aside and make the best of a bad situation, but she was a woman who didn't do anything halfway. When she gave, it was with her heart and soul.

Seth had the ability to crush both.

"You got what you wanted, Seth, and my father got his wish, too," she said quietly. "Half of the Golden M is yours, and we're married. There was nothing in that stipulation that stated we had to be friends, you know."

He crossed his arms loosely over his chest. "It would make the years ahead more pleasant, not to mention making things more comfortable for your daughter."

"Why would you care about Kellie?" she asked, bristling like any protective mother sensing danger for her cub. "For all I know, you hate her as much as you do me."

"I don't hate her, Josie." His mouth thinned in irritation. "She's an innocent child and had no control over the circumstances of her birth."

"You mean she had no control over her *parentage*, don't you?" She couldn't hold back the provocation in her tone.

"Yeah, I guess I do," he said, shocking her by candidly accepting her challenge. "Do you know who he is, Josie?"

A jolt of panic seized her, and her fingers curled around the armrests of her chair. His bold question ripped to the heart of her, and without thinking, she pressed a hand to her chest as if he were physically prying open a ten-year-old secret. She hadn't meant for things to go so far; she'd only intended to goad him and possibly anger him enough to put some much needed distance between them.

She was quickly learning that he wasn't a man easily diverted. From across the room, he appeared ruthless in his quest for the facts.

"Who's the father, Josie?" he prompted.

Knowing he'd never believe the truth and unwilling to drag her daughter into any resulting unpleasantness, she grappled for an ambiguous, sarcastic reply. "Why, Seth, I have no idea who the father might be," she said, tossing a flippant smile his way. "I slept with so many guys that just about anyone in your senior class could be a candidate."

He flinched as if her words had had the same impact as a slap across his face. Once he recovered from her offensive statement, his gaze narrowed and he studied her face intently, as though searching past the surface for clues she wasn't revealing. Dread and terror clashed within her. She didn't want to answer the new questions leaping to life in his eyes, didn't want to get trapped in a web of her own making.

Feeling extremely vulnerable under his scrutiny, she pushed away from her desk and stood. "I should head up to the house and get dinner ready," she said, scrambling for any excuse to gracefully bow out of the subject she'd brought up. She started toward the office door, but before she could escape, Seth reached out and snagged her arm, stopping her progress.

His fingers burned her skin; his eyes bored into hers. "It doesn't matter to me who Kellie's father is. What matters is whether your daughter harbors the same hatred for me that you do?"

How could he ask such a question after the way her daughter had taken to him? She searched his gaze, and beyond all the dark, angry emotions she'd provoked moments ago was something infinitely tender. Something kind and gentle she was powerless to resist.

Seth wanted her daughter's acceptance as much as Kellie wanted his.

Her heart tugged in two different directions. Ultimately, she couldn't bring herself to deny him, or her daughter, something so important. "No, Seth," she whispered, forcing back the tears rasping her throat. "Kellie doesn't hate you at all."

He slowly released her arm, letting his fingers gradually fall away from her sensitized skin. "Thank you," he said, and judging by the relief playing over his expression, she knew he meant it.

His finger paused just within his eyes traced line here. "It doesn't matter to me now, Kellie's father is. What matters is whether when she has babies likeness, better," for me, that you do?"

How could so ... that ... innocent me with his thought had been of numerous smothered his gaze with

CHAPTER SIX

JOSIE stared at the scene before her with a mixture of disbelief, shock and delight. The last of the three emotions was most prominent. It was also the most unwanted reaction to the wedding dinner her daughter had so painstakingly planned and created for her and Seth.

The kitchen nook had been transformed into a romantic haven for two. Josie's good linen tablecloth was draped over the dining table, and her fine china, crystal and silver made up two place settings at the nearest end. And it was difficult to miss the two taper candles rising amid a ring of handpicked roses and daisies, or the wedding bells made from construction paper and ribbon that hung from the light fixture over the table.

The smells wafting in the room were heavenly. Giving the kitchen a cursory once-over, Josie realized that Kellie must have taken the roast and vegetables she'd thrown into the Crock-Pot that morning before Seth had picked them up for their appointment with Reverend Wilcox and put them in the white scalloped covered dish. Sitting on the counter next to the main course was a decorative woven basket Josie used on special occasions; she peeked in the folds of the linen napkin and found the rolls she'd made earlier nestled inside.

She glanced over her shoulder at Seth, hoping he wasn't too uncomfortable with her daughter's enthusiastic display. He looked surprised by the scene, even a little overwhelmed, but not the least bit bothered by a young girl's fancy.

"It looks like Kellie has been busy this afternoon," Josie mused, impressed with her daughter's imaginative flair. She wasn't sure how she felt about the romantic atmosphere Kellie had created, especially since she was expected to share it with Seth.

"I think it's sweet and very thoughtful." Taking off his Stetson, he hung it on the hat rack by the back door and absently pushed his fingers through his hair. He came back to stand beside her near the table, his gaze warm when it met hers. "She's worked so hard to put everything together. Let's not ruin it for her."

In other words, he wanted her to pretend to be in the throes of wedded bliss, which was the furthest thing from the truth. She opened her mouth to tell Seth it was wrong to create such a false impression for Kellie when their marriage was born of practical reasons only, but before she could utter a word of her lecture, they were interrupted.

"Mom! Seth!" Kellie exclaimed. "I didn't hear you come in."

Both their gazes swiveled to the kitchen doorway where Kellie had come to an abrupt halt. She looked a jumble of excitement and nervous anticipation, and Josie couldn't bring herself to burst her bubble.

And so, for the sake of her daughter, she let the pretense of a happily married couple begin.

She gave Kellie a bright smile. "I'm sorry, honey, we didn't mean to spoil your surprise."

"That's okay." She smoothed a hand over the ruffled apron tied around the waistband of her blue jeans. "I, um, wanted to do something special for both of you. Since I didn't have time to buy you a gift, I thought I could make you a wedding dinner."

Josie's heart expanded in her chest. "This is lovely, Kellie."

"And certainly very special," Seth added in that deep, rich voice of his. "Thank you."

Embarrassed by all the praise, Kellie fluttered over to the

refrigerator, opened it and peered inside. "Why don't you two sit down and I'll get dinner on the table."

Seth stepped in front of Josie and held a hand toward her. "Shall we?" he inquired.

She stared at the callused palm he so gallantly offered, the long fingers that seemed to beckon for her to place her hand in his and trust him. Her mouth twisted derisively. Placing so much faith in him was something she'd never be so foolish as to do again.

It was silly to accept his assistance; their chairs were only a few steps away. But he wasn't backing down, which forced her to go along with his charade. Knowing the act was for Kellie's benefit, she placed her fingers against his palm. He led her to her seat, and just when he should have let go of her, he lifted her hand to his lips and placed a soft, warm kiss on the pulse point in her wrist.

Desire curled through her, and she valiantly fought the sensation.

His smile was shameless. "Enjoy the evening, bride. I'm sure many surprises lay ahead."

She wrenched her hand away and bit back a tart reply. The man was too bold and confident by half!

While she and Seth were settling into their seats next to one another and placing their linen napkins across their laps, Kellie filled three crystal goblets with iced tea.

"I think somebody is supposed to make a toast to the bride and groom," Kellie said.

Josie nearly groaned. Had her daughter taken notes from the wedding reception they'd attended last year?

"Why don't you do us the honor?" Seth suggested.

"Okay," Kellie agreed way too easily.

Seth passed a filled goblet to Josie, along with a warning look not to spoil the moment.

She gritted her teeth. As if she'd disappoint her own daughter!

The three of them lifted their drinks. Kellie looked from

one adult to the other, then her gaze settled on Seth, bashful but sincere. "I'm glad you married my mom because she's really special. I love her a whole lot and I want her to be happy and not so lonely anymore." Her voice trembled ever so slightly with nerves. "And I'm glad I have a dad now. I've always wanted one, and you're pretty nice."

Seth smiled gently at the compliment. Kellie clinked her glass to his, then to her mother's.

As far as toasts went, Kellie's was hardly eloquent or polished. As far as speaking from the heart went, her speech packed a wallop of emotions Josie understood all too well. Josie fought the sudden urge to cry. When had her baby become so grown-up?

Kellie set about bringing the food to the table, then lit the candles and turned off the light overhead. Though a low-wattage bulb burned over the kitchen sink, the glow of the taper candles cast a warm, soothing ambiance over the room.

Now that her job as waitress was done, Kellie inched toward the doorway leading back into the living room. "Well, I hope you enjoy your dinner."

"Where are you going?" Josie blurted, not wanting to be left alone with Seth and a candlelight dinner that was certain to be awkward and uncomfortable.

"I was going to go up to my room for a little while."

"I think you should join us." She must have sounded as frantic as she felt because an amused smile slowly curved Seth's mouth. She refrained, just barely, from kicking the rogue's shin under the table.

Kellie chewed her bottom lip uncertainly. "I thought you two would like to be alone."

Whatever had given her daughter *that* idea? Or was it wishful thinking on Kellie's part?

"There'll be plenty of time for us to be alone later," Seth interjected smoothly, though his intimation wasn't lost on Josie. He pulled out the chair next to him and patted the seat. "Come sit with us. This can be our first dinner together as a family."

Kellie's eyes brightened with pleasure. "Okay."

Josie had to admit that their wedding dinner was one of the most enjoyable experiences she'd allowed herself in a long time. She found herself relaxing in Seth's company. He made her daughter laugh and smile with silly anecdotes, and even had her joining in on the fun.

Too soon, the meal ended. Josie stood to clear the table, but Kellie popped up from her seat and motioned for her to sit again. Josie did so reluctantly.

"I have another surprise for you." Kellie looked giddy and ready to burst with her secret. "I'll be right back."

When Kellie disappeared into the pantry on the far side of the kitchen, she glanced at Seth. He shrugged, silently relaying that he didn't have a clue as to what the young, precocious girl had planned.

A minute later, Kellie stepped out of the pantry with a flourish, a beaming smile and a proud "Ta-da!" Held in her hands was a crystal platter with a crooked two-tiered cake on top. Slowly and carefully, she carried the treasured item to the table and set it in a spot between Josie and Seth, then returned to the cupboard for plates.

A smile twitched Josie's mouth. Her daughter had helped her bake on numerous occasions and now it seemed she had attempted to bake and decorate a wedding cake for her and Seth. While her effort was admirable, the result wasn't quite as attractive as a bakery-bought wedding cake. The double-layered confection leaned precariously to one side, making the small plastic girl and boy standing on the second tier—compliments of a miniature dollhouse set she'd gotten one year for Christmas—appear as if they were near to toppling over the side. The white frosting was lumpy, and Josie assumed that the blobs of frosting placed strategically on the cake were attempts at roses.

It was hilarious, and more touching than Josie could put

into words. Seth seemed moved by Kellie's sweet gesture, too.

Kellie cut the bottom layer of the cake, put two pieces on separate plates and handed one to each of them. "You're supposed to feed each other the cake," she said, and stood back to watch.

Seth lifted a dark brow, prompting Josie to explain, "Kellie saw it done that way at a friend's reception."

He picked up his slice of cake, his eyes lighting with mischief. "I'm game."

"Do it, Mom!" Kellie whispered from the sidelines.

Josie knew exactly what "it" meant—smash the cake into Seth's face, just as the bride had done to the groom at that reception. Kellie had thought that was great fun to watch and was apparently eager to witness the entertaining exchange again.

Debating for all of ten seconds the merits of turning a playful moment into a fitting retribution, Josie decided that Seth deserved every bit of the traditional wedding ritual.

They moved closer, bringing their cake up to the other's mouth. They both took a bite, and when he automatically lowered the uneaten portion of his cake back to his plate, she squished the rest of the cake in her fingers and smeared the sticky concoction along his mouth, jaw and cheek, giving him a white-frosting beard.

Seth reared back, his expression stunned, as if he couldn't believe she'd dare to do something so outrageous. Kellie cheered uproariously in the background, and spontaneous laughter escaped Josie. It felt wonderful to let loose.

Something in Seth's eyes changed, darkening with intent. Faster than she could anticipate, he grasped the hand coated with cake and frosting. A rakish smile lifted his lips, and she knew she was in big trouble.

Josie's heart slammed against her rib cage at the same time as an awful flavor filled her mouth. She blanched and stopped chewing. The cake tasted horrible, as if Kellie had added too much salt and not enough sugar to the batter. And the frosting had a bitter edge to it, enough to demand a drink of iced tea to wash it down.

If Seth realized how bad the cake tasted, he didn't show it.

"Okay, bride, let's see how you handle a dose of your own medicine," he murmured, his mouth softening with a smile that was warm, lazy, and just a trifle on the dangerous side.

Too late, she realized she'd provoked him too far.

He brought the hand coated with cake and frosting to his parted lips, the caress of his breath warming the tips of her fingers. Panic surged through her and her eyes widened...surely he didn't intend to take this to a sensual level with her daughter present!

The man had no scruples. Kellie believed his act was all innocent fun, but Josie knew better. Thank goodness only Josie was privy to the effect Seth's outrageous behavior was having on her senses.

Blue eyes glittering with a sexy, predatory heat only she could see, he slowly licked from the base of her palm and upward, lapping off the cake and frosting with the agile stroke of his tongue. She struggled for breath as a shocking jolt of excitement raced through her. She tried tugging her hand away; he tightened his grip.

"Umm, this has got to be the best cake I've ever tasted," he lied flagrantly, though Kellie was oblivious to his fib since he seemed to be enjoying the confection so much. "I'd hate for any of my slice to go to waste."

Kellie hooted, laughed and egged Seth on.

He came back for more, thorough in his sampling as he sucked a finger into his warm, wet mouth. The touch of his tongue slid between her sticky fingers and swirled around the tip, sending a wave of heat all through her and bringing a flood of color to her cheeks.

Her gaze beseeched him to stop. His gaze said she deserved every bit of the sensual torment. The silky interior of his mouth gave her pleasure. The sleek softness of his tongue made her tremble. The way he grazed his teeth along her fingers, then gently bit into the sensitive flesh just below her thumb made her gasp.

A shivery sensation rippled down her spine and settled in her belly. She felt dizzy with desire and an urgent need that startled her. His eyes were lit from within with a hungry, arousing fire that promised things she'd only experienced with him. Exciting, thrilling things she wanted to experience again—with him.

She moaned, and was horrified that she'd allowed the telling sound to escape.

She fought desperately to free herself of the drugging magic he created. Fought desperately to get herself, and the situation, back in control. If she let him triumph in this sexy game of wills, she knew she'd never stand a chance at winning the war she intended to wage in the bedroom that night.

It was that thought that spurred her into action. His hold on her hand had loosened, and this time when she tugged, her wrist slid free of his grasp. She reached for her iced tea and gulped down the rest of the cool liquid to wash away the unpleasant taste in her mouth. Then she beelined it to the sink to wash her hands.

Kellie sighed in the aftermath of the delightful moment and handed Seth a few damp paper towels so he could wipe the cake and frosting off his face. "I wish Grandpa was here," she said quietly, unintentionally putting a damper on the light atmosphere.

Josie knew her daughter was speaking from the heart. Kellie adored her grandfather and hated when he left for extended periods of time. This time, though, Josie feared Jake was gone for good, his guilt over losing the Golden M driving him away.

"I wish he was here, too, honey," Josie responded in an attempt to soothe her daughter.

"I miss him." Kellie's expression was sad and melancholy. "I hope he comes back soon."

Josie dried her hands on a towel, refusing to give her daughter false promises. She had no idea what her father intended, but considering he hadn't contacted her since last Friday when he'd gambled away the Golden M to an O'Connor she wasn't holding out much hope that he would arrive on their doorstep any time soon.

She glanced at Seth, who was watching the exchange with interest. There were questions in his gaze, but he didn't voice them.

She returned her attention to Kellie, deciding it was time to get things back on track. "Thank you for a nice evening, honey." A curly lock of hair had escaped her daughter's braid, and Josie gently smoothed the unruly strand away from her face. "It's been a long day for all of us, so why don't you go on up and take a bath and get ready for bed and I'll clean up the kitchen?"

Kellie nodded, suddenly looking tired. She took off her apron, smiled shyly when Seth thanked her for all her hard work on their dinner and wedding cake, then headed upstairs.

Seth stood and came up to the kitchen sink, using soap and warm water to rinse away any lingering frosting. The edges of his dark hair got wet in the process, and he raked the spiky, gleaming strands off his forehead with his fingers.

"Have you heard from your father?" Seth asked, patting his face dry with the hand towel.

"No, just the note you gave me." She stacked their dirty dishes and brought them to the counter, then returned to the table for more. "He gave me the impression that he's not coming back any time soon."

"I'm sorry, Josie," he said, his voice low. "I never meant for your father to leave."

She whirled around to face him. Her temper flared—anger, hurt and her own guilt over the situation clashing all at once. "What did you expect, Seth? He lost everything to an O'Connor."

"Not everything." His expression hardened, all traces of compassion vanishing. "You still have half of the Golden M, and that was a stipulation your father devised. He wasn't stupid about putting the Golden M deed into the pot. Both of us would win something, regardless of the outcome of our poker hands. His outstanding debts are paid, half of the ranch still belongs to his family, and I have a cattle ranch I intend to build into one of the top ten operations in the state of Montana." He pulled in a deep, calming breath. "Whether or not you believe me, I'm sorry that Jake is gone, but I can't and won't apologize for winning the Golden M."

They stared at one another, the air around them rife with tension. Josie guessed that the bitter emotions Seth had unknowingly injected into his speech were linked to the fact that he hadn't inherited any part of Paradise Wild. She wondered what had transpired between Seth and his father that would cause Seth to end up with nothing but a job on his family's ranch and a place to live. But he didn't look in the mood to talk about personal issues, and she decided she really didn't want to know the intimate details of his life, either.

He moved toward the back door and grabbed his hat from the rack. "I need to get Lexi's things put away down in the stables," he said curtly, jamming his Stetson back on his head. "I'll be a couple of hours, enough time for you to get ready for bed."

With that effective parting remark telling her what he expected from her when he returned, he was gone.

CHAPTER SEVEN

SHE was ready for Seth, cloaked in a physical and mental armor certain to put a damper on her husband's passionate intentions.

Josie smiled at her reflection in the dresser mirror, pleased with her appearance. It was the middle of summer, and normally she wore a thin, sleeveless, thigh-length cotton chemise to bed. In honor of her wedding night, she'd dug out her favorite old flannel gown she reserved for cold winter nights. The gown covered her from neck to wrist to ankle. She made sure every button was primly fastened all the way up to the ruffled collar at her throat, then donned a pair of matching pale pink socks so her feet were covered, too.

She giggled, unable to hold back the giddiness bubbling within her. Seth was so determined to have his wedding night, and she was going to give him one to remember. The flannel gown was as sexy as a potato sack, and as soon as she'd plaited her hair back into a severe, tight braid, she was certain that after he took one look at her, his interest would wane. And if he persisted in seeing things through despite her best efforts to look unattractive, then he was going to have to consummate their marriage with minimal cooperation from her.

This time, she would stay in control.

She heard the front door close and the lock click into place, and her heart fluttered uncontrollably in her chest. In a matter of minutes, Seth would be up in her bedroom, and she still needed to rebraid her hair. She'd meant to be in bed, snuggled beneath the covers, lights out, when he arrived.

Deciding that pretending to be asleep would have been the coward's way out anyway, she defiantly sat down at her vanity, took a deep breath to calm her nerves and began brushing her hair so she could plait it.

And anxiously awaited her husband's arrival.

Seth stepped into Josie's bedroom after making sure Kellie was in bed and asleep, his gaze drawn to the woman sitting at the vanity brushing her long hair. The light from the lamp on the nightstand shimmered off the curly strands, giving her hair a burnished, fiery luster he longed to sink his fingers into.

He closed the door, locked it, then moved purposefully toward her. She ignored him and continued with her chore. Setting the brush on the table in front of her, she separated her hair into three thick strands and began twisting them into a tight braid.

"Leave it down," he said, coming to stand behind her. It wasn't an order, but a polite request.

Finally, her gaze lifted, meeting his in the mirror above her vanity. She didn't stop the quick movements of her hands and fingers as they continued weaving. "My hair is prone to tangles," she responded flatly.

He never figured she'd make tonight easy on him, knew she'd do her damnedest to defy him, but he wasn't about to let her thwart him. Not in the bedroom.

"Don't waste your energy on this fight, Josie," he said meaningfully. "I want your hair down." This time, his tone was demanding enough to make her glare at him with fire in her eyes. Pushing her hands away, he used his fingers to comb through the silky strands. Her hair was long, thick and luxurious. The curly tresses clung to his fingers, slid sinuously over his hands. His body quickened, making him realize just how much he wanted her. How determined he was to have her.

Still standing behind her, he took off his Stetson and set

it on her vanity, boldly claiming his right to be in her bedroom. In her life. As husband and lover. Then he pulled his T-shirt from the waistband of his jeans, drew it up and over his head, then tossed it aside, leaving his chest bare.

She watched him in the mirror, more out of rebellion than any compelling urge to see him strip off his clothes. He unfastened the buckle cinched at his waist, slowly slid the strip of leather through the loop of his jeans and placed the belt next to his hat. Still her gaze remained cool and distant.

Allowing a slow, wicked smile to claim his lips, he popped free the top button of his jeans. Her breath caught at his brazenness, and her fair complexion flushed with indignation. Or maybe excitement, he mused.

Satisfied that he'd finally gotten a real feminine reaction out of her, he spared her the immediate embarrassment of him stripping off his pants and having her see the full effect she had on him. He was fully aroused, and he'd yet to do any of the things to her that he'd fantasized about all day long.

Moving to the large four-poster, he sat on the edge of the mattress. "Come here, bride," he said, softening the command with a charming smile. "I need your help to take off my boots."

The searing look she shot him told him what she thought he could do with those boots of his. "Can't you take them off yourself?"

Bracing his hands behind him on the bed, he reclined casually. "Oh, I've managed just fine for the past twenty-nine years. I just thought this would be more fun."

Her gaze narrowed skeptically. "You have a warped sense of what a person considers 'fun'."

"Aw, c'mon, Josie darlin'. Don't be such a stick in the mud." Unable to resist goading her, he added, "It's not like I'm asking you to get naked." Not yet, at least, he thought.

With an audible, perturbed humph, she accepted his challenge and stood, giving him his first full-length glimpse of what she was wearing. He blinked. Twice. Then he frowned.

The ugly, unflattering gown she was wearing engulfed her entire body, concealing everything feminine about her, from the lush swell of her breasts, to the sweet curve of her waist and hips, to the sleek line of her thighs and calves. And she was even wearing socks, for crying out loud!

He didn't know whether to laugh or be irritated. "Flannel?" he questioned incredulously.

She gradually approached him. The long gown swirled around her ankles and billowed around her slender form like an oversize burlap bag. "What's wrong with flannel?"

"In case you haven't noticed, it's the middle of summer." His tone was openly sarcastic. "Not to mention our wedding night."

Stopping beside the bed where he was sitting, she lifted her shoulders in a shrug. "It's soft and comfortable."

His gaze flickered down the length of her. "It's hideous."

A felinelike smile curved the corners of her mouth. "That's an added bonus, too."

He chuckled, unable to help himself. Did she honestly think an uncomely flannel nightgown would stop him from making love to her? In his estimation, she wouldn't be wearing the garment for long, so it didn't really matter what it looked like at all.

He crooked his finger at her. "C'mere so we can get my boots off," he suggested easily, then maneuvered her so she was standing in front of him, her back to him. "The way to get the best leverage is to let me put my leg between yours and you grab the heel of the boot. One good hard tug and it should slide right off."

She stiffened when he wedged his leg between hers, offering her his boot, but she didn't complain or back down.

The hem of her gown lifted with his leg, giving him a fascinating view of her limbs to her shapely thighs. Giving in to temptation, he leaned forward and caressed that silky skin.

She sucked in a sharp breath, jumped forward out of his reach, then twisted around to scowl at him. "Keep your hands to yourself, O'Connor."

He affected an innocent, little boy expression and held his hands up at his sides. "Okay, darlin'," he drawled, knowing there would be plenty of time for touches later. But first, he needed to get Josie to relax and loosen up. "Give my boot your best effort."

With an admonishing look not to further distract her, she turned back to her task. He flexed his foot when she yanked, and the boot slid off. She repeated the process with his other boot, then quickly moved away from him, shaking out the voluminous skirt of her gown until it covered her decently again.

He pulled off both his socks and put them with his boots. "Now how 'bout you take off your nightgown?"

"I prefer to keep it on," she said, moving around the bed to the other side.

He stood facing her from across the wide mattress they would share and jammed his hands on his hips. He refused to get mad with her tonight, no matter how much she prodded him. "Josie, sweetheart," he said, his tone soft and infinitely patient, "either you take off the nightgown, or I'll do it for you. One way or another, it's coming off."

Her answer was to pull back the spread and blanket on her side of the bed, slide in between the covers and yank them up to her chin.

Stubborn woman, he thought, blowing out a harsh breath. Fine. Two could play her game. Unzipping his jeans, he hooked his fingers into the waistband and pushed the heavy material down his legs. Leaving his briefs on for the time

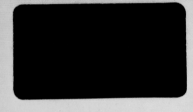

WELCOME TO THE
CASINO:

Try your luck at the Roulette Wheel ...
Play a hand of Twenty-One!

How to play:

1. Play the Roulette and Twenty-One scratch-off games, as instructed on the opposite page, to see that you are eligible for FREE BOOKS and a FREE GIFT!

2. Send back the card and you'll receive TWO brand-new Harlequin Romance® novels. These books have a cover price of $3.50 each in the U.S. and $3.99 each in Canada, but they are yours to keep absolutely free.

3. There's no catch. You're under no obligation to buy anything. We charge nothing — ZERO — for your first shipment. And you don't have to make any minimum number of purchases — not even one!

4. The fact is, thousands of readers enjoy receiving books by mail from the Harlequin Reader Service® before they're available in stores. They like the convenience of home delivery, and they love our discount prices!

5. We hope that after receiving your free books you'll want to remain a subscriber. But the choice is yours — to continue or cancel, any time at all!

So why not take us up on our invitation, with no risk of any kind. You'll be glad you did!

Play Twenty-One For This Exquisite Free Gift!

THIS SURPRISE MYSTERY GIFT WILL BE YOURS FREE WHEN YOU PLAY TWENTY-ONE

It's fun, and we're giving away *FREE GIFTS* to all players!

PLAY ROULETTE!

Scratch the silver to see that the ball has landed on 7 RED, making you eligible for TWO FREE romance novels!

PLAY TWENTY-ONE!

Scratch the silver to reveal a winning hand! Congratulations, you have Twenty-One. Return this card promptly and you'll receive a fabulous free mystery gift, along with your free books!

YES!

Please send me all the free Harlequin Romance® books and the gift for which I qualify! I understand that I am under no obligation to purchase any books, as explained on the back of this card.

Name: _____
(PLEASE PRINT)

Address: _____ Apt.#: _____

City: _____ State: _____ Zip: _____

Offer limited to one per household and not valid to current Harlequin Romance® subscribers. All orders subject to approval.

PRINTED IN U.S.A.

316 HDL CQX3

116 HDL CQXH
(H-R-08/99)

The Harlequin Reader Service® — Here's how it works:

Accepting your 2 free books and mystery gift places you under no obligation to buy anything. You may keep the books and gift and return the shipping statement marked "cancel." If you do not cancel, about a month later we'll send you 6 additional novels and bill you just $2.90 each in the U.S., or $3.34 each in Canada, plus 25¢ delivery per book and applicable taxes if any.* That's the complete price and — compared to the cover price of $3.50 in the U.S. and $3.99 in Canada — it's quite a bargain! You may cancel at any time, but if you choose to continue, every month we'll send you 6 more books, which you may either purchase at the discount price or return to us and cancel your subscription.

*Terms and prices subject to change without notice. Sales tax applicable in N.Y. Canadian residents will be charged applicable provincial taxes and GST.

being, he joined her and moved close. In one swift move he tossed the spread and sheet down to her sock-clad toes.

Her mouth pursed, but she didn't scramble for the covers. "Would you turn off the light, please?" she asked primly.

Bracing himself on a forearm, he stared down at her. "I prefer to keep it on," he said, mocking her by repeating her own words.

She opened her mouth to protest, and he pressed his fingers to her lips. They were soft and damp and he couldn't wait to taste them. "Don't argue, Josie. If you insist on keeping the gown on, then I insist that the light stays on." He lifted a dark brow. "Care to change your mind?"

"No," she said, the one word vibrating against his fingertips.

The resolute emotions he saw radiating in the depths of her eyes should have put him on alert, but he was confident that just like the day he'd kissed her in the kitchen, he could make her want him again. Despite everything that had happened in the past, despite everything that stood in the way of their future, there was a chemistry between them that burned like wildfire when they touched. He wanted to lose himself in that heat, wanted her to be with him all the way.

He slid his fingers from her mouth and along her cheek, savoring the satiny texture of her skin, then buried his hand in her luxuriant, vibrant hair until his palm cupped the back of her head. Her lashes fluttered closed, and she lay unresponsive and slack. The one arm nearest him was pressed against her side and his chest, and the other was crooked so her hand rested by the side of her face. Her fingers curled slightly inward, giving the impression that she was totally relaxed. Asleep even.

He knew better. She was attempting to feign disinterest, and that was something he wouldn't tolerate when he knew just how responsive she could be. He lowered his head, settling his mouth over hers in a soft, gentle kiss. She didn't resist his advance, but neither did she participate. He added a subtle pressure, and her lips automatically parted to receive his tongue, allowing him to deepen the kiss. He swirled, dipped and cajoled, but she didn't join in on the seductive foray, just let him have his way with her mouth. He could have been sucking on a peach for all the involvement she mustered.

He lifted his head and stared down at her impassive face. Her restraint was admirable, but annoying as hell. It also spurred him to more ruthless measures. Keeping his fingers tangled in her hair, he continued to kiss her, the slow, deep, intimate kind designed to entice and arouse. He slid his open mouth along her jaw, her neck, tasting his way to the sensitive spot just below her ear.

He thought he felt a shiver ripple through her but couldn't be sure since she showed no outward enjoyment of his seduction. But she would, of that he was certain.

He distracted her with gentle love bites along her throat while deftly unbuttoning the front of her gown to her waist. He slid his hand inside the opening over her collarbone, skimmed slowly downward, then heard a sharp, surprised gasp catch in her throat.

He lifted his head and smiled at the firm set of her jaw. Ah, his bride wasn't as indifferent as she tried to let on. Stroking his palm along her warmed skin, he parted the flannel, exposing one plump breast that swelled and tightened as he watched. He rasped his thumb over the tip, and it instantly hardened. Unable to stop the deep, needy groan rumbling in his chest, he dipped his head and nuzzled the fragrant hollow between her breasts, dragged his open mouth along one slope and drew a taut nipple into the hot, wet depths of his mouth.

The hand at the side of her head curled into a tight fist, and her breathing deepened, making her chest rise and fall rapidly. Still she didn't move, didn't touch him, didn't respond the way a woman should when her body was so obviously in tune with her lover's. Her expression remained emotionless.

The first stirring of discontent gripped him, but he refused to admit defeat so early. "You're determined not to enjoy this, aren't you, Josie?" he accused mockingly.

She didn't answer, but he didn't really expect her to. She'd managed to withdraw mentally from the situation, but he took some satisfaction in the fact that she hadn't been able to shut down her physical response to him.

Taking advantage of that one small concession, he purposefully moved his hand over her flannel-clad hip down to her thigh and slowly dragged the hem of her gown upward until he had the material bunched around her waist.

He'd managed to unveil most of her body, baring her lush breasts and the sleek length of her hips and legs. He smiled grimly. She could issue no justifiable protest of his indiscreet actions, either; she was still wearing the blasted gown!

He realized he would have welcomed any verbal sparring over this kind of complacent behavior.

He brushed his fingers over her flat belly, and her flesh quivered beneath his touch. Pleased with that small victory, he lifted his gaze to her face to watch for an emotional response and leisurely trailed his fingers lower. Tracing the edge of her cotton panties around to her hip, he slipped his hand inside the elastic band and glided his warm palm over her smooth bottom. He gave the flesh a gentle, kneading squeeze.

She bit her bottom lip, and the pulse at the base of her throat throbbed wildly.

He gritted his teeth, his irritation mounting. Shifting closer, he pushed his hard thigh between hers, making her legs part to make room for him, though he didn't move completely over her. Lifting one of her legs over his hip, he added a rhythmic pressure to that sensitive, feminine haven. Slow and easy, he rocked against her, mimicking the motions of a more intimate joining. Desire coiled low in his belly, and he grew impossibly hard with wanting her.

She arched toward him subtly and whimpered, then valiantly swallowed back the sound.

He swore, at her, at himself, at the situation. He didn't want a wife who merely accommodated him for the sake of appeasing his baser needs. He wanted Josie to ache the way he ached. He wanted her to be as uninhibited as she'd been eleven years ago, holding nothing back. As selfish as it was, he wanted all the passion he knew she was capable of giving. All of her heat. All of her desire. Unconditionally. Freely. Openly. And until he had her on equal terms, needing him as much as he needed her, he didn't want her at all.

A low growl of frustration rumbled in his chest, and he pushed himself onto his back and rested a forearm over his eyes, breathing slow, steadying breaths in an attempt to cool his libido and his temper. The longer he lay there and contemplated the situation, though, the angrier he became. He'd been gentle and willing to give Josie every pleasure, and she'd outright rejected him!

Abruptly, he rolled back onto his arm so his body was pressed against hers, so she could feel the evidence of his desire. Taking her chin between his thumb and forefinger, he turned her head toward his.

"I know you're not sleeping, Josie, so open your eyes," he said with a forced calm, though his voice was laced with enough steel that she obeyed.

Her lashes drifted open, her eyes a bright shade of green. "What?" she questioned softly, as if she was the injured party in this debacle of a wedding night.

Her demure act made him even more furious, and he managed, just barely, to hold his escalating temper in check. "I've never had to force you to make love before, and I'm not about to start now. You won this round, Josie, but tonight is nothing but a brief reprieve. We *will* make love, and the next time I'll expect your full cooperation.''

She didn't utter a word, but then she didn't have to. Her gaze all but snapped with defiance.

He smiled, and played his trump card. ''Keep in mind, Josie darlin', this marriage isn't legal until we consummate it. And in order to consummate our union, it's going to take *both* of us participating.''

Her feisty rebellion dimmed; it was obvious she hadn't considered everything she stood to lose by being so uncooperative in their marriage bed.

Deciding to let her sleep on that, he yanked the sides of her nightgown together to cover the temptation he wouldn't be enjoying that night and pulled the rest of it back down into place. He turned off the lamp on his nightstand, then returned to her, circling an arm around her waist and tucking his still-aroused body along hers. She tensed but didn't complain or struggle away.

Sleep was a long time in coming for both of them.

He'd underestimated Josie's ability to remain unresponsive, and that rankled Seth more than he cared to admit. He'd gone to sleep in a surly mood, though getting a few hour's rest hadn't improved his disposition any. He'd slipped out of bed before the crack of dawn, taken a much needed cold shower, then headed down to the stables, not wanting to be anywhere near Josie until he'd decided what to do with his stubborn bride.

Saturday it had been easy to avoid her. A fence was down in the west end and it had taken the day to put it to rights. Seth had joined in on the repair, as much to give Mac and the other men an extra pair of hands as to show his employees that he had no qualms about working hard on the Golden M. What he expected of his hands, he expected of himself, and he'd proved at least that much with his efforts, gaining their respect in the process.

He stayed out on the range even after the other hands had headed in for the day, herding stray cattle and familiarizing himself with the boundaries of the Golden M. The sense of rightness had calmed him somewhat, but not enough to diminish the unsettling emotions from the previous night's escapade.

When darkness forced him to return, he'd spent more time than necessary cleaning tack. Kellie had brought him a plate of meat loaf, vegetables and rolls for dinner and chatted with him while he'd eaten. He'd enjoyed her company and had to smile when she'd told him that she'd smuggled the food out to him. Apparently when Kellie had expressed her concern about his not showing up for supper, Josie had told her when he was hungry enough, he'd come in and fix his own meal.

At least he had an ally in Kellie.

When he'd finally returned to the main house hours later, the place had been dark and quiet. Kellie was in bed, and when he entered Josie's room, he'd found her huddled beneath the covers, pretending slumber. He'd taken a long, hot shower, slipped into bed without putting any briefs on and snuggled close to Josie. She'd been wearing that dreaded flannel again, but he was too exhausted to engage in a battle for her to take it off so she could gradually get used to their sleeping skin to skin.

She'd flinched when he'd pulled her against his chest, gasped and attempted to squirm away when he'd brazenly cupped his hand over her breast.

"Settle down, Josie," he'd murmured in her ear. "I'm too tired to demand my husbandly rights tonight." It was an out-and-out lie, considering how a certain part of his anatomy had eagerly leaped to life the moment he'd touched her.

He'd spent the entire night like that, and this morning's routine had been no different than the previous one. Up early. Cold shower. Out of the house before Josie woke.

He'd skipped breakfast, and his stomach was growling fiercely, reminding him that he was a man who liked three hearty meals a day. Midmorning was rapidly approaching—soon he'd be forced up to the main house to slap together a couple of sandwiches.

Something had to give between him and Josie—and he felt as though he'd given plenty and for the most part exhibited the patience of a saint where Josie was concerned. He was willing to set past grudges aside, so why couldn't she at least meet him halfway? Or was she trying to make his life so miserable he'd ask for a divorce and forfeit the Golden M to her?

"Not a chance, sweetheart," he muttered to himself. No way would he give up something that offered him so much security and a future he alone had the power to shape. He'd lived under the pressure of his father's thumb for more years than he cared to remember, then endured his brother's manipulations, as well.

He was finally his own man, broken free of the O'Connor influence and domination. Freedom certainly tasted sweet.

Stabbing his pitchfork into a pile of straw, he evenly distributed the pieces into the stall he'd just cleaned out for Lexi. Briefly, he wondered what Josie planned to do today, Sunday, then just as quickly told himself he didn't care.

Booted steps echoed down the corridor in the stable, and Seth stopped moving to listen. The gait was slow but firm, not the clipped, efficient sound he'd come to associate with Josie's steps. He was irritated to realize he was disappointed.

Stepping outside the stall, he saw Mac casually strolling down the aisle. The foreman glanced into an occupied stall and doled out a treat to the horse within.

Seth frowned, not in the mood to fraternize with anyone. "What are you doing here?"

"Howdy, boss," Mac said congenially, then gave another mare a slice of apple along with an affectionate rub on her snout. "Just checkin' on things, like I do every Sunday afternoon for Josie."

"There's no need for you to do that any longer." Seth appreciated the man's loyalty, but he was more than capable of handling any problems that arose. And he'd be right on hand, considering he spent most of his time in the stables. "Take the day off and spend it with your wife."

Mac crooked a graying brow his way. "You should be doing the same."

Seth's smile was halfhearted. "My wife doesn't want *my* company."

A grin split the older man's weathered face. "Uh-oh, trouble in paradise already?"

Seth's answer was a plain and simple grunt of disgust. He wasn't willing to elaborate beyond that.

Mac, however, had no qualms about pursuing the issue. "Considering your grouchy mood yesterday, I figured your wedding night didn't go as planned."

Seth blanched inwardly. Great. Had his sex life, or lack thereof, been the topic of discussion yesterday when he hadn't been around? "Just leave it alone, old man." Not caring for the direction this conversation was heading, he propped his pitchfork against the stall and headed toward the tack room.

"Seems to me you don't know the ways of women," Mac offered absently as Seth stalked past. "Especially one like Josie."

Seth came to an abrupt stop and whirled around. All the emotions that had accumulated over the past week—frustration, anger, bitterness—finally boiled over. "Oh, I know Josie all right," he said, his voice heated with resentment. "Better than you or anyone else thinks!"

Mac took off his aged leather hat and slapped it against his thigh, calmly digesting that information. "I suppose what's between the two of you is really none of my business—"

"No, it's not," Seth said succinctly. The last thing he wanted, or needed, was someone meddling in his relationship with Josie.

"But I'm going to tell you what I think anyway."

Seth ground his teeth and told himself to walk away, but something kept him rooted to the spot.

"Josie has been through a lot in the past ten or so years," Mac began, stepping up to the next stall to give the mare within her share of attention. "She's had a child on her own and raised that little baby into a sweet young girl. She's endured remarks about Kellie's parentage, and she doesn't date because men expect more from her than she's willing to give, if you know what I mean."

Seth knew exactly what Mac meant, but he wasn't to blame for Josie's past indiscretions. "What does all this have to do with me?"

"Maybe it has more to do with you than you think." He cast a casual glance Seth's way. "The two of you were seeing each other some years ago, weren't you?"

Seth's body tensed at the question, but he saw no point in lying about the gossip that had circulated around town. His father's anger over Seth's involvement with Josie had overridden discretion, and after a few drinks, anyone within earshot had heard David O'Connor grousing about his son making time with Josie McAllister.

"Yeah, we spent some time together," he admitted.

"She was pretty shook up when you broke things off."

Seth scoffed at that. All he'd seen from Josie the past week was a cold, frosty heart. But there had been a time when she'd been warm and sweet.... "What happened between us wasn't just about me," he said, annoyed that he felt the need to defend himself over what had clearly been Josie's duplicity. *She'd* used *him*, not the other way around!

"No?"

Seth didn't care for the other man's penetrating stare.

"No," he stated firmly. "There are circumstances you obviously don't know about."

"Maybe," Mac said vaguely.

Seth jabbed a finger in the foreman's direction. "Don't make me out to be the bad guy."

"Oh, I don't think you're the bad guy at all," Mac conceded. "But you shouldn't be heapin' all the blame at Josie's feet, either."

Seth's impatience climbed a few notches. "You're talking in riddles, man, and making little sense."

Frowning, Mac absently scratched his head. "That tends to happen when the years creep up on you."

Seth didn't believe the foreman for a second. Mac was old but sharper than a tack. Was he insinuating that there was more to what happened between him and Josie than met the eye? Seth shook his head. The old man had no idea what had transpired eleven years ago! Had no idea that Josie had slept with him in an attempt to claim him, an *O'Connor*, as the father of her child. It was a sick sort of vengeance, but she hadn't denied any of it.

And he'd paid a steep price for that brief time with Josie.

Scrubbing a hand over his jaw, he blew out a heavy breath that did nothing to ease the tightness in his chest. "If you're done with your Sunday sermon, I'd like to finish what I'm doing." He again started down the corridor.

"Be gentle with her," Mac said.

Seth halted and turned around, compelled to reply. "Doesn't work. I've tried it."

Filching another wedge of apple from his shirt pocket, Mac held the treat out to a mare bobbing her head over a stall. "Breaking a stubborn filly takes time, doesn't it?"

Seth squeezed his eyes shut for a moment, unable to believe Mac was actually comparing Josie to a filly, of all things! "And it's up to me to break her?" he guessed wryly.

Mac shrugged, a smile playing around his mouth. "So

to speak. Just like a skittish filly, you need to give her time to trust you're not going to hurt her. You need to woo her."

Woo her? Seth thought cynically. "She's my wife," he said, as if that fact excluded him from such nonsense.

The look Mac gave him was direct and wise. "It doesn't make her any less a lady, and all ladies like to be courted and romanced. Do it properly, and you'll tame your little filly without breaking her spirit."

Seth crossed his arms over his chest, doubting Mac's frivolous idea. It would take more than hand-holding and pretty words to smooth things over with Josie. His filing for divorce would certainly do the trick, but that wasn't an option.

Settling his hat back on his head, Mac nodded at Seth as though they'd just conducted business. "I'll be on my way now. Have a good day, boss."

Seth doubted that would happen, either.

CHAPTER EIGHT

SETH pulled his truck out of the parking lot of Pete's Hardware and made a right turn through town and toward the Golden M. He'd spent the past two hours picking up supplies and running errands, having decided that the next couple of days he'd devote to the business end of the ranch rather than use the daylight hours working the range. Eventually, he'd balance the two separate duties, probably committing his mornings to helping his men in any capacity they needed, and the afternoons in the office and around the main house.

When he'd told Josie of his plans that morning at breakfast, she hadn't seemed pleased that he'd be underfoot and invading her personal space in the office. He felt no guilt over crowding her businesswise; they had a ranch to run, and he knew at least in that area he'd get more cooperation from her than he had in the bedroom. She had the Golden M's best interests at heart and wasn't the type to let any of the daily business slip by her. She'd shared the financial information with him when he asked, even went over schedules, sales and other accounts, and she did it all in a very efficient, professional manner.

He could have been dealing with a stranger rather than his own wife, for all the emotion she'd exhibited.

Seth shook his head in frustration and gripped the steering wheel, irritated that one particular woman had the ability to tie him up in knots—not that he'd ever let his exasperation show in front of her.

It was three days into the following week and his bride was no warmer than she'd been on their wedding night. Oh, she was polite enough when they were in the same room with one another, or when a particular need or subject forced them into conversation, but she didn't go out of her way to be gracious.

The days out on the ranch with the hands flew by with incredible speed; the nights were endless and frustrating. He hadn't attempted to make love to Josie again, and his bride didn't seem inclined to instigate any intimacy, either.

They were at a stalemate.

As much as he'd scoffed at Mac's suggestion on Sunday to woo Josie, Seth was seriously beginning to ponder the merits of courting rituals. If a few romantic gestures eased his strained relationship with Josie, then maybe it was worth taking the extra time and effort to make her feel special.

He mulled over his conversation with the foreman as he cruised by the main shops in town. In a more rational mood than he'd been on Sunday, he was better able to analyze Mac's not-so-absurd idea.

Maybe, just maybe, he'd come on too strong on their wedding night and expected too much, too soon. Women were inclined to be sentimental about their first night with their husbands, and he supposed, despite the uninterested act she'd put on, Josie was no different. In fact, remembering back to their time together, he recalled her enjoying the simpler things, nonsensical things, really…like a walk in the woods, frolicking in the creek or picking berries and feeding them to him.…

Seth tried not to think of those occasions because those sweeter times with Josie conflicted with her perfidy. And if he intended to make this marriage work, there was no room for past resentments to get in the way of their new relationship. They'd both grown and changed over the years, matured into adults who possibly shared a certain amount of regret for what happened eleven years ago.

He knew he regretted the way he'd handled the situation. And now, he hadn't taken Josie's feelings into account.

She'd been thrust into this predicament so suddenly, without warning or enough time to adjust to the idea of becoming his wife. Was it really fair of him to expect her to be warm and willing without giving her any reason to?

It wasn't the sex that was so important, but the bonding and intimacy that came with making love. He and Josie needed to establish that link in order to make a good, solid marriage. And in order to make it good in bed, he needed to gain her trust.

He needed to woo his stubborn filly.

Glancing into his rearview mirror and scanning the businesses lining the sidewalks on either side behind him, he made a spontaneous decision that had him making an illegal U-turn in the middle of the two-way street.

He was going to buy his wife some flowers.

Josie heard Seth's truck pull into the driveway, and continued the boring task of filing paid invoices in the metal cabinet next to her desk. He'd been gone most of the afternoon, thank goodness, giving her a brief reprieve from his wholly male presence that had dominated her small office that morning.

She couldn't concentrate on her work when he was near and preferred the days when he tended to the outdoor tasks on the ranch. From his grand plan to split his time between the day-to-day operations of the Golden M and the business and paperwork end, it was obvious that she was going to be spending more time with Seth than she cared to. She wondered how she'd survive—her office space was limited, yet designed to be efficient for one person to maneuver around in. Not two, as the time they'd spent together this morning had proved. The accidental way he'd brush by her, the way he'd lean close to get a better view of what she was working on, and the way he spoke in a lazy, sexy drawl, all combined to ignite a sizzling awareness that made her feel like a young schoolgirl again.

She heard him get out of the truck and his boots crunch on the gravel outside, then echo in the stable and down the corridor to her office. Her heartbeat accelerated, and she resolutely told herself that she was *not* eager to see her husband.

Shaking off the hum of anticipation warming her blood, she stuffed a paid bill from Pete's into the appropriate file and picked up a statement from the veterinarian. It was getting more and more difficult to remain aloof with Seth, mainly because he no longer took her indifference personally. Or if he did, he didn't show it in front of her. He acted as though there was no dissension between them, as though the past, present and future were not tangled in discord. His pleasant, friendly behavior totally threw her off balance.

She heard him pause at the open office door, and the hairs at the back of her neck tingled, and her skin suddenly felt too tight beneath her soft faded jeans and plain cotton blouse. The awakening of feminine senses was immediate, disturbing and thrilling in a way that was dangerous.

She resumed filing and waited for him to say something or walk into the office. Seconds seemed to tick by, and then he knocked, a light rapping of his knuckles against the woodframe. She frowned, instantly suspicious—Seth never knocked!

Determined to maintain her bland, detached attitude, she stayed where she was. "You must have purchased some manners while you were in town," she couldn't resist commenting offhandedly.

His amused chuckle was rich and deep and filled the room with warm, masculine tones. "The manners came free of charge with the flowers I bought for my bride."

Certain she'd misheard him, she finally turned around to face him. "Excuse me?"

He stepped into the office and strolled toward her, carrying in the crook of his arm an arrangement of long-stemmed white roses, baby's breath and delicate ferns all

tied together with a frilly white bow. Reaching her, he held
the beautiful bouquet out for her to take.

Her mouth went dry, and she gawked from the glorious
offering, to his amused expression, then back to the floral
display.

He tilted his head, a smile teasing his mouth. "What's
the matter? You don't like roses?"

Snapping out of her shock, she took the bouquet, cradling the precious flowers in her arms so she wouldn't
crush any of them. Pleasure rippled through her, as sweet
and heady as the fragrance she inhaled. A burning sensation
pricked her eyes, and she knew she was close to making a
fool of herself over something as stupid as roses.

She'd never, ever received flowers before.

"What are these for?" she blurted, refusing to let her
emotions get the best of her.

"For you," he said simply.

"Why?" She couldn't help the suspicion in her tone or
the slight narrowing of her eyes.

He merely grinned. "Because Mary Jo at the florist's
looked like she could use some business today, and I felt
sorry for her."

She gave in to temptation and touched a rose petal, mar-
veling at the silky texture. "They must have cost a small
fortune."

"Cost wasn't a factor."

How could such an ordinary statement make her feel so
cherished, so special? Her throat tightened with more emotion, and she swallowed it back. Dammit, she didn't want
him to be nice to her! She had no defenses when he was
being so sentimental and charming.

He tipped his hat back on his head, blue eyes sparkling
with mischief. "So, when a husband gives his wife flowers,
doesn't he at least get a kiss in return?"

His request startled her, heating her cheeks, exciting her
on levels she didn't want to acknowledge. "A bribe?" she

asked in an affronted tone, playing along with his cat-and-mouse game. "Is that what this is all about?"

"It's about you and me, and courting my bride."

Her pulse raced at the dare in his eyes. Her stomach clenched at the prospect of kissing him...because she suddenly wanted that and much more. Rising on tiptoe, she leaned toward him and gave him a tentative, chaste kiss on the cheek. The deed was done and over with in less than a heartbeat.

"Is that the best you can do?" he drawled, his voice taunting and husky at the same time.

All she had to do was say yes to end their game, but the word wouldn't come. She'd been aching for him since their wedding night and she suddenly lost the urge to deny herself something she wanted so badly.

She wanted to kiss her husband.

He didn't make it easy on her. Didn't angle his head or bend a little so she wouldn't have to strain up to meet his lips. A tad annoyed with his uncooperativeness—which ironically reminded her of her own lack of participation a few nights ago—she shifted the roses in her arm so they wouldn't get crushed and moved closer until her body brushed his.

An arm slid around her back—gentle, supportive and in no way demanding. He cradled her tenderly, careful of the bouquet, careful of her.

He waited for her to initiate the kiss, his eyes dark and hooded. Heart pounding erratically, she slid her free hand around to the nape of his neck, lifting her mouth while pulling his head down to hers.

Their lips met, warm and soft, sliding sinuously, gradually parting for a deeper taste. She took what he offered, coaxing him to participate, and when he did, she gave to him freely, without reservation.

Hunger exploded between them, and she arched closer, opening her mouth wider beneath his. He groaned low in his throat. The kiss turned very passionate very quickly, both of them meeting the other halfway, like a kiss should. It was a ravenous kiss that changed all the rules she'd established for herself, for them...an insatiable kiss that melted her resistance and set her on fire with a need that was as startling as it was arousing.

And Josie knew in that moment that she could never go back to being cold and unresponsive. The possessive look glimmering in his eyes when they finally ended the kiss told her he knew that, too.

"I, um, thank you," she said breathlessly, her entire body tingling from their kiss and his thoughtful gesture.

He dabbed his tongue on his bottom lip as if savoring the taste of her still lingering there. "For the flowers or the kiss?"

She surprised herself by saying, "For both."

"You're welcome, Josie darlin'," he drawled huskily. A grin curved his lips and lit up his eyes, and something magical happened between them in that moment. "For both."

Seth's attentiveness didn't end with the flowers. The next two days were filled with fleeting touches that brought Josie to a fever pitch but ultimately left her wanting. And the slow, heated glances he cast her way were designed to make a woman weak in the knees.

It certainly did the trick for her.

Seth was infinitely kind and considerate, playful and irresistibly engaging. Unable to ignore his charming attempts to forge a truce, Josie found herself responding in a similar fashion, and the end result was a tentative building of friendship.

They worked in harmony down in the office, and up at the house they'd struck an accord, too. Watching him tease Kellie while they ate their meals, hearing their laughter mingle, would be enough to give any outsider the illusion that they were a happy family. But Josie knew the problems

between her and Seth had been merely put aside in defer-
ence to their making the best of a difficult situation, and
certainly not one forgotten or resolved.

They slept in the same bed every night, Josie donning
flannel, Seth immodestly stripping down to nothing but a
glorious body honed by hard, physical work. The only thing
he asked of her was a good-night kiss, nothing more. But
oh, what a kiss it was—seemingly longer, deeper, more
seductive than the previous night's.

That one tantalizing kiss after a day of enduring subtle
caresses and sexy innuendos was enough to inflame her
senses. But he didn't take advantage of her soft moans of
delight, didn't demand any more intimacy than the joining
of their mouths, the mating of their tongues.

What once was relief at being left alone was gradually
being replaced by acute disappointment. How could he kiss
her so passionately and not take that coaxing seduction to
its logical conclusion?

*It's not as though you made it easy for him on your
wedding night*, a little voice reminded her. It seemed a lifetime ago, when in fact it had only been a week. And as
much as she wanted Seth, she knew she was better off
without establishing that deeper level of intimacy between
them. She was already softening too much where he was
concerned, enjoying their time together more than was
wise, considering his selfish, single-minded reason for marrying her.

Josie pushed those disturbing thoughts from her mind.
Standing at the kitchen sink, she rinsed breakfast plates and
loaded them into the dishwasher while Kellie and Seth
cleared the table. Once Kellie finished her morning chore,
she went to change for the day, leaving Josie alone with
Seth.

She was elbow-deep in soapy water, latching onto the
skillet to scrub when he came up behind her, settled his
big, warm hands on the curve of her waist and trapped her

against the counter with the easy press of his hard body along hers.

Her breath caught in her throat, then she released it in a long whoosh. "Seth..."

He nuzzled his face against her neck, his lips soft and damp where they skimmed her sensitive flesh. "Mmm, you smell good enough to eat," he murmured. "Like strawberries."

The mental picture his words projected in her mind caused her breasts to swell and her nipples to tighten. "It's, uh, my hair. I washed it this morning." Her shampoo smelled like wild strawberries.

Flattening a hand on her stomach to keep her close, he lifted his other hand and threaded his fingers through the silky, curly tresses rippling down her back. "Did you leave it down for me?" he asked, his voice low and sexy.

Yes. She swallowed hard and struggled to maintain her composure. "No, I left it down so it could dry before I braided it."

He pressed his mouth closer to her ear. "If I asked you to leave it down for me today, all day, would you?"

A shiver raced down her spine, settling where his hips tucked so snugly against her bottom. "It'll get—"

"Tangled," he finished for her, though his tone wasn't angry, just amused. "I'd be happy to brush the tangles from your hair and braid it for you tonight before we go to bed."

Her hands went slack in the soapy water at his intimate proposal. How in the world would she endure such sensual torment? The gentle tug of his pulling a brush through her hair, feeling his hands sift through the heavy strands, stroking along the nape of her neck...

"I'll clip it back," she said, the only compromise she was willing to offer.

He sighed, the sound teeming with feigned inconvenience. "I suppose that's fair enough." She heard a smile in his voice, and knowing he couldn't see it, she smiled in return.

"Mom!" Kellie called from the living room, dispelling the romantic, relaxed mood Seth had so easily woven. "Someone in a blue van just pulled into the driveway!"

Josie frowned. She lifted her hands from the cooling water and dried them just as Seth moved away from her. She didn't know anyone who drove a blue van. Thoughts of her father automatically entered her mind, along with the hope that he'd come to his senses and returned. She quickly headed toward the foyer with Seth following behind her.

By the time she met up with Kellie, who now stood out on the front porch to greet their visitor, a short, dark-haired woman was stepping from the driver's side of the minivan.

Josie didn't know the woman personally—they'd never been introduced formally—but she knew at a glance who she was. Erin O'Connor, Jay's wife.

"Erin!" Seth sounded as surprised as Josie felt. "What are you doing here?"

The pretty woman smiled and cheerfully waved up at the three of them. "I came to congratulate my brother-in-law and his new wife on their marriage. That, and the kids have been pestering me all week to visit their uncle Seth." She opened the back sliding door to the van, and two kids jumped out.

"Uncle Seth!" two voices rang out in unison.

Both kids raced toward the house. The young girl held the lead, her soon to be longer legs eating up the distance. The little boy, who appeared to be the younger of the two, struggled to keep up with his sister's longer stride.

Seth grinned and headed down the stairs, meeting the energetic children halfway. Squatting, he caught both of them as they flew into his arms, nearly knocking him off balance.

He laughed and gave them each a big hug. "I've missed you guys," he said.

A huge smile wreathed the little girl's face. "We've missed you, too."

He tugged on one of the girl's brown braids and ruffled the boy's dark head of hair. They beamed from his attention. "You two been staying out of trouble?"

"We always stay out of trouble," the girl said primly.

Seth lifted a dark brow. "Then how come your nose is growing?"

Her blue eyes widened and she touched her nose to be sure it was still small and pert. Her relief was visible. "You big tease!"

Seth winked at her. "Yeah, but for a minute there you weren't sure, were you?"

The boy snatched Seth's Stetson and put it on his own head. The brim fell over his eyes, and he pushed it back so he could peer out at his uncle. "Where's Lexi?" he asked.

"She's down in the stable." Running a hand through his dark hair, Seth straightened. "Maybe in a little bit I'll take you to see her, and you can feed her an apple."

Josie watched the exchange from a distance, feeling too cautious to join the group. Kellie stood beside her, seemingly waiting to follow her lead. Erin had made her way to Seth and the kids, her friendly smile still on her face. Josie kept waiting for Jay to appear from the other side of the van—the anticipation of a confrontation had her stomach clenching.

As if reading Josie's mind, Seth asked, "Where's Jay?"

"He had some business to take care of in town that will take up most of the afternoon," Erin replied easily.

Seth's gaze remained steady on his sister-in-law. "Does he know you're here?"

"No, but I plan on telling him." There was a hint of defiance in her voice.

Seth's expression turned grim. "You probably shouldn't."

"I'll handle Jay, Seth," she said confidently. "Besides, he's going to have to get used to me visiting you sooner or later. We're still family."

Seth absently scrubbed a hand along his jaw, showing his frustration over the issue. "Yeah, I know that, but Jay is having a harder time accepting that fact."

Erin didn't comment on that, probably because there was nothing she could say to refute Seth's statement. Instead, she glanced up at Josie. "So, do I get to meet your new wife and my new niece?"

"Of course." Seth led the way up to the porch, the kids tagging along behind.

Josie took a deep breath and summoned a smile, though it wavered on her lips. She realized she was nervous because more than anything she wanted this woman's acceptance. It was silly, really, but a fact nonetheless. Josie had few women friends, and if Erin was inclined to forge a friendship, even a tentative one, Josie was willing to meet her halfway.

Seth made the introductions, and Josie shook Erin's hand, which was warm and welcoming.

"I'm pleased to meet you," Josie said automatically.

"Me, too," Erin replied, her eyes sparkling. "I've always wanted a sister, and now I've got one." Then she said a few words to Kellie and made her feel like part of the family, too.

Josie instantly liked the other woman—it was obvious Erin didn't harbor the same adverse feelings toward a McAllister as her husband did. But then again, the bitterness of the feud hadn't been as ingrained in her as it had Seth and Jay.

Seth brought his niece and nephew forward to be introduced. "This here's Brianna, who's six, and this cowboy here is Brendan, and he's four."

Both children handled the introductions with a politeness that made Josie smile.

"Uncle Seth, do you have a ball we can play with?" Brianna asked, already bored with grown-up manners.

"I do," Kellie offered, excited at the prospect of having someone to play with, even though her cousin was four years younger. "I'll be right back." She disappeared into the house, and Brianna and Brendan headed down the stairs to frolic on the lawn.

"Why don't you sit down and relax?" Josie offered, waving a hand toward the two wicker chairs set up in the right alcove of the porch. "And I'll go get some refreshments." They'd just eaten breakfast, but Josie knew the kids wouldn't refuse a cookie or a glass of lemonade.

Ten minutes later, she returned, balancing a tray with a pitcher of cold lemonade, plastic glasses and a plate of homemade cookies. All three kids were kicking the ball back and forth between each other out on the grass, their peals of laughter ringing in the air. Josie smiled at how well the children were getting along—a new generation not yet totally influenced by the enmity between their families. She couldn't help but wonder if the kids would continue to be friends, or would they one day realize that there was a dividing line they dare not cross?

Pushing that depressing thought aside, she set the refreshments on the wicker table in front of the two chairs. Sliding into the empty seat opposite where Erin sat, she listened as Erin brought Seth up to date on the problems Jay was experiencing now that Seth was no longer working on the Paradise Wild.

"You were his best hand," Erin said plaintively. "Now that you're gone, it's as though the rest of his men don't know what to do. You held it all together out in the field."

Seth leaned casually against the porch railing, crossing his legs at the ankle. "Then Jay needs to spend more time working side by side with his men instead of staying cooped up in the office. He's got to balance the two."

Erin nodded in agreement but didn't look convinced.

"I've tried to tell him that, but he's not in a mood to reason."

"He blames me for the problems, doesn't he?" Seth asked knowingly.

Reluctantly, Erin nodded. "He's been as grisly as a bear since you, um..." Her gaze flickered to Josie, then back to Seth.

"Married Josie?" Seth offered.

She cringed in embarrassment. "Well, yes. The word 'traitor' has come up in conversation a few times," she added with wry humor.

Seth laughed, but the sound lacked any real amusement. "Yeah, I know Jay sees things that way. But what Jay doesn't take into consideration is that there was nothing for me on Paradise Wild, no incentive, and certainly no future. I don't wish my own brother anything bad, but neither do I regret what I've done. I've got a fertile piece of land, a solid cattle business and prime stock."

Josie listened to Seth, her heart aching in her chest. She, along with the Golden M, was only an acquisition to him. Nothing more. Just part of the package her father had so considerately offered him. It hurt. She didn't want it to matter, didn't want emotions to become intertwined in their business proposition, but somehow, for some reason, she was beginning to care.

"I know Jay wanted to join the two properties again and make it all O'Connor land, but it's not going to happen." Seth glanced at Josie, his gaze softening immeasurably before he shifted it back to Erin. "This is Josie and Kellie's home, too, and I'd never do anything to jeopardize that."

"That's the way it should be," Erin said, compassion in her tone. "Your first loyalty should be to your new family."

"I'm glad I have your support, but I don't think Jay is quite as understanding." His mouth stretched into a grim line. "If Jay doesn't do something about all that bitterness that's been festering for years, it's going to destroy him just like it destroyed our father. It's already caused strife between the two of us, and we're the only family each other has left.''

Erin sighed and brushed her dark hair away from her face. ''I know you're right. It might take time, but I'm working on him, Seth.''

Seth nodded but said no more.

''Uncle Seth,'' Brianna called from the lawn, ''can we go feed Lexi an apple like you promised?''

When Seth hesitated, Erin waved a hand in dismissal. ''Go on,'' she urged. ''Us girls will be just fine without your presence.''

Josie watched Seth join up with the kids and head down to the stables. Suddenly, she felt uncomfortable sitting with Erin, a woman she barely knew. She had no idea what to say, couldn't think of an appropriate subject for them to discuss on the heels of the conversation Erin had just had with Seth.

Erin easily smoothed over the awkward silence that had fallen between them. ''Looks like you and Seth are settling in quite nicely,'' she commented.

Josie inwardly grimaced. If only Erin knew how rough the past week had been! ''Yes, all things considered.''

A knowing smile touched Erin's mouth. ''I take it you're referring to the rift between the families?''

Feeling the need for something cool and refreshing, Josie poured them each a glass of lemonade, admitting, ''Never would I have ever imagined marrying an O'Connor.''

Erin accepted the drink Josie handed her and took a sip. ''But you and Seth once dated, didn't you?''

Josie eyed the other woman, her new sister-in-law, and wondered what rumors she'd heard about her and Seth and the slew of other guys she'd reportedly been involved with. Seeing no condemnation in her gaze, she relaxed. As for ''dating'', theirs hadn't been a traditional courtship. ''We spent some time together in high school, yes, but…things didn't work out."

"Why not?"

Erin's straightforward manner was both heartening and unnerving. Josie wondered how her sister-in-law would feel if she tarnished her image of Seth with the facts—that he'd used her for his own purposes eleven years ago. "The feud between our families got in the way," she said vaguely, though that was a large part of the truth.

Erin reached for a cinnamon sugar cookie and nibbled on it. "You know, I always thought that feud between the two families was silly, really. I mean, a McAllister won a parcel of land from an O'Connor. Certainly a McAllister shouldn't be condemned for holding a winning hand."

Josie managed a smile. "Well, there's a lot of speculation about Grady McAllister cheating."

"Bah! If he'd cheated, the land never would've been legally deeded to him."

"True, but the O'Connors haven't quite seen things that way." Leaning back in her chair, Josie sipped her lemonade, enjoying Erin's company as well as her understanding of the longtime feud. Why couldn't the rest of the O'Connors have been so reasonable? "It's been a vendetta for over seventy-five years now. And with each generation, the bitterness just seems to get worse."

"Maybe your marriage to Seth will finally put an end to it." She sounded hopeful.

"That all depends on Jay." Taking into consideration that the man they were discussing was Erin's husband, she chose her next words carefully. "He's not very fond of me or my family. And now that Seth has been forced to marry me, it's only caused more friction between the brothers."

Erin arched a brow. "'Forced' is a strong word."

"Seth certainly wouldn't have chosen me for a wife."

"He doesn't look miserable to me."

Erin hadn't been around the first couple of days when

misery had been the overall mood on the Golden M. "We're working on a compromise."

"That's what marriage is all about." Erin paused for a few seconds as if weighing the wisdom of interfering in Josie's marital affairs, then forged ahead. "Seth is a good, honorable man, Josie, even if you believe otherwise. The kind of man who will stand by you in good times and bad."

Josie thought back to eleven years ago when Seth *hadn't* been so honorable. But at the beginning of their relationship, he'd seemed the perfect gentleman, so sincere and certainly forthright in his pursuit. Her judgment of his character had failed her then, and her pride had taken a tremendous blow. Yet now, eleven years later, she saw the same gentlemanly traits in Seth—characteristics she had begun to believe in and trust.

She was beginning to feel so confused, about the past, the present, and certainly about Seth's intentions!

"And if it makes you feel any better," Erin continued, oblivious to Josie's inner turmoil, "the problems between Jay and Seth go a lot deeper than just his marriage to you. But that's something the two of them need to work out between themselves when the time is right."

"And if that time never comes?" Josie asked hesitantly.

"Oh, I'm certain it will," Erin said confidently. "You see, I've been an impartial bystander in this rift between the O'Connors and McAllisters, and though I'm totally devoted to Jay, I'm not blind to his faults and weaknesses." Her gaze traveled out to the stables, where Seth and the kids had gone, as if seeking a certain person. "Over the years I've put a few pieces of an intriguing puzzle together, bits I've learned and overheard, and I've come to a startling conclusion. Now I'm waiting for someone else to realize the truth that's staring him in the face."

A shiver tumbled down Josie's spine, settling in her stomach like a rock. She was too stunned by Erin's cryptic statement to respond, but Josie's mind registered the shocking fact that Erin must know the truth she'd managed to keep secret for ten long years.

"It's just a matter of time, and a matter of trust, I suppose, before everything comes together," Erin said, glancing back at Josie with a sad smile on her face. "And when the realization hits home, it'll either tear the family apart for good, or it'll finally put an end to a seventy-five-year-old feud."

CHAPTER NINE

"LAST one to reach the creek has to do the dinner dishes tonight!" Kellie announced gleefully from atop her mare, Juliette.

Josie and Seth glanced at each other from astride their own horses, and Seth watched a playful twinkle enter his bride's eyes that lit up her entire face.

She exchanged a mischievous look with Kellie and accepted the challenge, which put Seth into the competition, too. "You're on!"

A grin splitting her face from ear to ear, Kellie spurred Juliette across the green pasture and toward the shimmering stretch of water half a mile away. Josie was right behind her daughter, leaning low over her horse's neck to gain maximum speed, leaving Seth to pull up the rear.

Not that he minded. Quite the contrary, while technically he'd be the loser of the race, he was winning in so many other ways. The view from behind was extremely alluring. As she bent over her mare, Josie's spine was straight, tapering into a curvy waist and a heart-shaped bottom snuggled in her saddle. But it was her glorious hair that captured his complete attention.

Ever since that day in the kitchen nearly a month ago when he'd commented on her leaving her hair down, she'd gradually modified the way she wore the long, wavy tresses, as if slowly, unconsciously, she was allowing herself to accommodate him, her husband. Leaving it unbound wasn't always practical, but she didn't always opt for a braid, either. Most of the time she clipped the mass behind her, at the base of her neck, so he could still finger the silken strands.

Today, she'd taken the hair around her face and secured it with a barrette on top of her head, leaving the rest to fall over her shoulders in a luxurious array of spiral curls. As she rode her mare, the wind whipped through the tresses, the strands rippling behind her like cinnamon fire and spun gold. Every night, she left her hair down as he requested, and he'd spend what seemed like endless hours running his fingers through their incredible softness, stroking those lustrous tresses until she fell into a deep slumber.

Her smiles and laughter were becoming a regular occurrence, too…like now, her throaty chuckles filling the air, wrapping around him and settling warmly in the pit of his belly. But there were times when she didn't realize he was watching her that her expression reflected a heartbreaking sadness. He'd yet to figure out what was bothering her so much. At one time, he wouldn't have cared…but he was discovering that Josie's happiness was somehow interlaced with his own. And when she was feeling gloomy, it hit him on a level that made him feel protective and extremely possessive.

He was falling for Josie, his stubborn bride, hard and fast, despite all the turmoil of the past and regardless of the fact that beyond the friendship they were forging, she hated him for stealing away half the Golden M and trapping her in a marriage she didn't want. And there wasn't a damn thing he could do about his growing feelings for Josie except keep them tucked away so she couldn't use those vulnerable emotions to manipulate him. He didn't like to think that history would repeat itself, but he wasn't willing to take any chances and give her that much power over him.

Kellie and Josie brought their mares to a smooth stop a few yards away from the creek. After sliding out of their saddles, they jogged to the edge of the water, both laughing and breathing hard from the ride and warm sunshine.

Kellie pointed at Seth and did a merry dance as he brought Lexi to a stop next to the other horses. "You're the big loser," she said jovially.

"Oh, yeah?" Dismounting from Lexi in one fluid motion, he dropped the reins so the horse could graze, then sprinted toward Kellie. She squealed in surprise and darted in the opposite direction, with Josie egging her on.

Seth caught her and gently tackled her to the soft grass. He tickled her with fast, sure fingers, unmerciful in his attack.

"Stop! Stop!" she demanded around peals of laughter and gulps of air.

Seth grinned and continued the playful torment, finding all the places that made her break into fits of giggles. "Who's your favorite guy?"

"You are!" Kellie was forced to confess.

Satisfied with her admission, Seth stood and held out a hand to help her up. "And don't you forget that, either," he said with feigned gruffness.

"You're a lightweight, Kellie," Josie said with a grin. She still stood near the creek, enjoying the scene before her and making the mistake of thinking she was safe from Seth's attention. "You gave up way too easily."

"I had to say it!" Kellie pressed a hand to her aching side. "I couldn't breathe!"

Seth stalked toward his bride, slowly and predator-like. "Do you think I'm a loser, too, Josie?"

Casually, she inched away from the edge of the creek. A smile quirked the corner of her mouth, and her eyes shimmered sassily. "Oh, absolutely."

Like a lithe cat, he unexpectedly leaped toward her. Her eyes grew round in panic and she had just enough time to whirl away, but Seth was faster and more agile. He caught her around the waist with a strong arm, but instead of tumbling her to the ground, he swept her up into his arms and strode purposefully back to the creek.

She gaped at him, her expression reflecting a mixture of disbelief and uncertainty. "You wouldn't dare!"

"I'd dare just about anything, Josie darlin'," he drawled.

She squirmed in his embrace as they neared the crystal blue water. "You can't be serious!"

A slow grin curved his lips. "I'm about as serious as that water is cold."

She stiffened, sliding her arms around his neck as if to hold on for dear life. He couldn't deny that she felt like heaven snuggled that way against his chest.

"Seth!" she admonished.

He stopped at the edge and met her gaze. "Who's your favorite guy?" he asked, his tone low and taunting.

Defiance sparked from her eyes. "Mac."

He chuckled at her rebellious behavior. "Wrong answer. Try again."

She closed her eyes for a brief second, as if it pained her to say the words. He prompted her by loosening his hold, just enough to make her suck in a panicked, outraged breath and cling to him.

This time, her admission came swiftly. "You are! You are!"

"Do you mean it?" he murmured.

She glanced down at the glittering pool of water beneath her and obviously thought better of her answer. "Yes!"

Finally, he released her, letting her body slide down the length of his until her booted feet touched the ground. Keeping his hands secured on her hips, he angled his lips near her ear. "I'm gonna make you prove it later on."

Her cheeks flushed a becoming shade of pink.

"Aw, Mom," Kellie groaned in disappointment as she trudged over to the adults, "I can't believe you gave in."

Josie stepped around Seth, severing the contact between them. "I'm not in the mood for a swim."

Seth shared a grin with Kellie. "Where's your sense of adventure, bride?"

"I must have left it back at the house," she retorted, and added under her breath, "And quit calling me that!"

He would, as soon as her status changed from bride to wife. He used the endearment as a constant reminder that they'd yet to consummate their marriage, and she knew it, too.

He'd been patient the past month, giving her time to get used to him and the thought of their being together intimately. He touched and kissed her at every opportunity, and it was getting more difficult to end the petting and caresses before they escalated beyond the point of no return. He took satisfaction in knowing that Josie was becoming just as restless as he was and more often than not initiated a kiss or touch of her own.

He was ready to make love to her, ready to make her his in every way a man longs to claim his woman, his bride. But it wouldn't happen, not until Josie was ready, physically and emotionally.

Soon, he thought.

While Josie spread a blanket beneath a nearby shade tree and retrieved the knapsack tied to Lexi's saddle, which held their picnic lunch, Seth taught Kellie to skip stones along the surface of the water. The three of them ate ham sandwiches, potato chips, cookies for dessert, washing it all down with lemonade. Their conversation was lively and fun, and the hour passed languidly.

After the remnants of lunch were cleaned up, Kellie rolled up the hem of her pants to her knees and waded into the shallow end of the creek to pitch more stones. Josie relaxed against the trunk of the tree, legs stretched in front of her. Stomach full and feeling wonderfully relaxed, Seth removed his Stetson, reclined on his back and rested his head in her lap. She appeared startled by his bold move, but she didn't object, and gradually the tense muscles in her thighs eased.

Sighing contentedly, Seth smiled up at her. "I can't think of a better way to spend a Sunday afternoon."

"Me, neither," she said softly, her gaze taking on that melancholy look he'd yet to understand. "My father and I used to take Kellie out for rides and picnics on Sundays when he was around...."

Her voice trailed off and she grew quiet. A faraway look touched her expression, and he finally realized what evoked such sadness in her at times. Her father's absence.

"I hope he's okay, wherever he is," she said, more to herself than to him, he suspected.

Grabbing her hand, he placed it over the steady beating of his heart. The tender gesture was meant to comfort her and maybe show her, in his own simple way, that he did care. "Has he ever taken off before?"

She nodded, the movement jerky. "Yes, but never for this long. I'm afraid he won't be back this time." Emotional tears filled her eyes, but she managed to keep them at bay. "He was a good man, Seth, despite his faults."

"I never thought differently."

She drew a deep, steadying breath. "It was common knowledge that he liked to gamble, and I tried my best to keep it under control, but he became obsessed with cards and poker after my mother died when I was a little girl. I suppose it was his way of dealing with her death, and I'd much prefer him gambling than drinking."

"Like my father?" It wasn't an accusation, just a statement of fact.

"Yes," she agreed, lightly brushing a strand of hair off his forehead. "It couldn't have been easy for you."

He laced his fingers with the hand he held to his heart. "No more or less than it was for you." Both of them had suffered as children, though in different ways.

She hesitated for a brief moment. "I heard rumors that he was...um, a mean drunk."

Seth valiantly tamped the old resentments and bitterness clawing their way to the surface. "My father was just plain mean and spiteful, regardless of his drinking."

"I'm sorry." Compassion glinted in her eyes, soothing him. "My father's got a heart of gold and deserves to be home with me and Kellie." She closed her eyes and swallowed hard, her voice wistful when she next spoke. "I wish..."

When Josie didn't finish, Seth prompted, "What do you wish, sweetheart?"

She opened her eyes, and they were bright with private recriminations. "That my father knew that I forgive him for gambling away the Golden M, and that I don't hate him like he believes. But how can I tell him that when I have no idea where he is or how to find him?"

Seth had no answer for her, but he didn't think she expected one, either. Her request was such a simple one, really, and as they sat there together beneath the shade tree lost in their own thoughts, Seth decided if it was within his power to grant Josie her selfless wish, he would do it.

"Mom, there's a wild berry bush a little ways down the creek," Kellie said, skipping back to the blanket. "Can I pick some so we can have them with ice cream tonight?"

"Go ahead," Josie said with a smile as Kellie took an

empty container from the knapsack. "But stay where I can see you."

Seth closed his eyes, lulled by the warmth of the summer day, the soft, feminine scent drifting off Josie's skin, and the way she idly stroked her fingers through his hair. A nap beckoned, and he gradually drifted off.

"Seth?"

Josie's soft, sweet voice tugged at his consciousness, keeping him hovering between slumber and wakefulness. "Hmmm?"

"What happened to make your father disinherit you?"

His mind immediately went on full alert, but he didn't open his eyes. "It doesn't matter."

"I'd like to know, considering that's the main reason why you wanted the Golden M so badly."

His lashes drifted open, and he gave her a warning look. "Leave it alone, Josie." His tone was gruffer than he'd intended, but he hoped it would at least serve to dissuade Josie from probing into a very sensitive topic.

She fell silent but wasn't discouraged for long. "Did Jay do something so your father would disinherit you?"

His jaw clenched, and he admitted, "No, it was what *I* did."

She frowned as if she couldn't quite believe he was capable of doing something so awful that it would result in the loss of his rightful inheritance. "Which was?" she persisted.

"Dammit, Josie..." Frustration burned through his veins, along with truth, until it threatened to strangle him if he didn't let it out. "I was with *you*."

Visibly shaken by his confession, her hand fluttered to the collar of her blouse and her face paled. "My God."

Swearing heatedly beneath his breath, he sat up next to her on his knees. He clawed his fingers through his hair, angry with her for pushing the issue and equally furious with himself for having so little restraint. "You wanted to know," he said, his tone flat.

Her eyes searched his, compassion glowing in their depths. "You lost half of Paradise Wild because of me?"

"Because of *us*." He ached to touch her and tell her it no longer mattered, but he couldn't bring himself to open himself to her so emotionally. "Because I was involved with you and my father found out about it."

She squeezed her eyes shut. "And because I'm a McAllister," she stated, her voice holding a hint of anguish.

"That's the long and short of it. It was no secret my father hated anything McAllister."

She looked at him, her chin jutting out indignantly. "That's awful, and hardly fair!"

He felt himself smiling because never would he have imagined having Josie as an ally. "Life is rarely fair, Josie, as you are well aware. My father always knew something happened between you and me, but I didn't find out about being disinherited until after my father died, when the will was read."

She shook her head. "You must have been devastated."

He shrugged, the gesture not as casual as he intended. "At first I was pretty angry, but then, that's my father for you. Spiteful until the very end. But none of that matters anymore. This is my home now, here on the Golden M, with you and Kellie."

She drew her legs up and wrapped her arms around her knees. "Not by your choice."

"No, the circumstances weren't ideal, but we're both in this for the long haul, and I've accepted that."

She cast him a skeptical look beneath the crease of her brow. "And the past?"

"Has no place in our future," he said adamantly. "I...I care for you, Josie, and Kellie, too. I know we can make our marriage a good one if we work really hard at it."

She glanced away from his beseeching gaze, but not before he saw something extremely emotional and private glittering in her eyes, as if she was trying to hide a secret from him. Very gently, he grasped her chin and brought her face back around, but whatever he'd glimpsed moments before was gone.

"I'm willing to wipe the slate clean. How about you?" he asked, realizing in that moment just how important her answer was to him. How important it was to their marriage.

She bit her quivering bottom lip. A month ago, she would have been snapping with fire right now, defiant and unwilling to compromise. He was gratified to see her relenting, softening, and giving consideration to everything they stood to gain as true, equal partners—in marriage, friendship and business.

Since she was having a difficult time agreeing to what he wanted, he decided to offer her an incentive. Framing her face between his large palms, he leaned toward her and kissed her tenderly, deeply, passionately. "Say yes, Josie," he breathed against her damp lips. "Say you'll be my wife."

Tentatively, her arms slid around his neck, fingers delving into his hair, and brought his mouth back to hers. "Yes," she whispered, and then her lips parted beneath his. The kiss she gave him tasted like a new beginning and held the flavor of forever.

Yes. Seth's heart soared. That one word was all he needed to hear to know she was finally his.

It took Josie a week to work up the nerve to seduce her husband. After her declaration at the creek last Sunday, she'd expected Seth to make love to her, but he'd been a perfect gentleman, in their bedroom and out. He still kissed her every night until she was pliant and dewy, still stole caresses that left her breathless and murmured sexy, wicked things in her ear that made her blush. The anticipation he so effortlessly stirred within her was excruciating, but exquisitely sensual.

Wanting him was driving her crazy.

She knew she was sending all the right signals, but it had taken her the whole week to realize Seth was waiting for her to initiate a more intimate union between them—when she was ready.

The time had come to be Seth's wife in every way, as she'd promised him at the creek, and there wouldn't be a more perfect opportunity to make her intentions known than that evening. Kellie was staying overnight at a nearby friend's house, leaving her and Seth alone on a quiet Saturday night. Seth had gone out to the stables an hour earlier to check on things, as he did every evening, affording Josie enough time to prepare herself, physically and emotionally, for what was to come.

She'd never considered herself a seductress—she knew little about tempting men—but as she glanced at her reflection in the dresser mirror, she saw a mature woman who was both desirable and sexy. She supposed trading in her long flannel gown and socks for a silky, thigh-length chemise and bare feet had something to do with the transformation, as well as leaving her hair completely unbound so it fell in wild curls over her shoulders and down her back. Her complexion glowed, and her eyes shimmered with feminine allure.

She was as ready as a bride could be to accept her husband for the first time.

Downstairs, she heard Seth enter the house, and she

started as the moment of reckoning presented itself. Excitement and apprehension mingled, making her pulse race and her stomach flutter from nerves. Like a repeat of their wedding night, she anxiously waited for him to come upstairs, and when she finally heard his booted steps echoing down the hall, she drew a deep breath for calm and courage.

The door opened, and he stepped inside, his gaze immediately drawn to where she stood in the middle of the room. He said nothing, but his dark, smoldering eyes spoke volumes. They leisurely traveled the length of her, flickering from her unrestrained hair, to her breasts that swelled and pushed against the cool material of her chemise, to her hips outlined in silk and down her slender legs. His perusal was blatantly seductive and wholly possessive.

This time, she didn't attempt to repress her body's response to his heated gaze. This time, she didn't bolt for the safety of the covers and wish that the lights were turned off. This time, she let him look his fill, let the hunger between them grow and build until she was inflamed and restless.

There would be no holding back tonight, no barriers, and that knowledge sent a thrilling shiver of anticipation dancing down her spine.

"Hi," she said, her voice husky.

"Hi yourself." Taking off his Stetson, he flicked it onto the nearby dresser. He strolled lazily toward her and stopped less than two feet away. "You look awfully nice and sexy without all that flannel covering you up." His gaze narrowed and his voice lowered into a masculine, teasing drawl. "You expecting someone I should know about?"

She shifted anxiously on her bare feet, and the silky material of her gown whispered around her thighs, a teasing caress she wanted his hands to replace. "Just my husband."

One corner of his mouth tipped up in a beguiling, rakish grin. "And now that he's here, what do you plan on doing with him?"

Her pulse quickened at the shameless challenge in his eyes. Taking a step closer, she closed the gap between them and sank her fingers into the soft hair at the back of his neck. "Maybe I ought to show you," she said, and brought his mouth down to hers.

She kissed him, no holds barred. Deep. Passionate. Ravishing. His lips were infinitely soft, incredibly warm, his tongue flirtatious as it chased hers. She couldn't get enough of his taste, didn't want the kiss to end.

Too soon, it did, though she wasn't the one who put a stop to such a toe-curling experience. It had been her husband, and he was looking down at her with unbridled hunger burning in his eyes.

His finger traced the thin strap holding up her gown, then trailed a heated path along the bodice to where it dipped between her breasts. "Dressed as you are, and kissing me that way, you're asking for trouble, bride."

She knew what he was asking—did she realize what she had in store if she continued this game? "I'd say I'm *looking* for trouble, cowboy," she said, and began slowly undoing the buttons on his shirt.

He watched her perform the task, not touching her the way she wished he would, and the ache within her grew. She fumbled with a particularly stubborn button and tried not to let her self-confidence wither. Tonight was very important to her. Not only did she want to please him, but she wanted to show him that she was willing to meet him halfway, willing to do her part to make their marriage work.

And it all started here, tonight, in their bedroom.

Finally, the sides of his shirt separated, and she slipped her flattened palms inside, gliding over hot flesh that seemingly quivered from her touch. Impatiently, she pushed the material over his shoulders and down his arms, breathing in a warm, male scent that made her dizzy with longing. She greedily explored his hard and firmly muscled chest, discovering the man he'd become, indulging in the changes in his body, reveling in her own womanly response. She brushed her fingers down his belly but was stopped by the waistband of his jeans. A sound of frustration rose in her throat before she could stop it.

Soft, intimate laughter rumbled from his chest. "Slow down, Josie darlin'," he murmured. "We've got all night."

He didn't understand the excruciating tension swelling inside her, the exquisite pressure she needed to relieve. Her breasts were full and achy, her stomach quivering, her skin hot and tight. She needed...

"Touch me," she whispered, expressing her greatest need.

His eyes glowed with a primal brilliance. "Show me where you want me the most."

Feeling no hesitancy with him and not allowing any inhibitions to intrude on their night together, she took his hands and pressed his open palms to her breast. "Touch me here," she said in a barely audible voice. She was certain he could feel her wild heartbeat, certain he could sense her escalating desire. "Touch me everywhere."

He rasped his thumbs across her silk-covered nipples, and she closed her eyes and moaned in pure pleasure. She shivered when his mouth skimmed her throat, swayed against him as he strung damp kisses along her neck, automatically parted her lips for him as he settled his mouth over hers for a languid, seeking, devastatingly thorough kiss.

And then his hands wandered, touching her everywhere as she'd asked. His fingers glided over her belly, over her trembling thighs, stroked along her back, then circled around to grasp her hips and pull her close. Even through silk and denim there was no mistaking how much he wanted her.

The heat and friction was more than she could stand. She whispered that she couldn't wait, and he growled in response, moving her back toward the bed. He stripped off her chemise and didn't stop touching her until he'd charted every bare inch of skin. Somewhere along the way, he'd managed to tug off his boots, his socks, and hastily shed his jeans and briefs.

She only had a handful of seconds to admire his well-honed body before he was gently pressing her onto the mattress, then following her down. Automatically, her legs parted for him, and he settled himself in between. Thrusting his fingers into her hair, he angled her mouth more firmly beneath his, and she returned the kiss with eleven years of accumulated passion, need and desperation.

And then he was pushing inside her, his hips rocking urgently against her. A sharp gasp caught in her throat at the burning sensation spreading within her, and she arched and wrapped her legs around his hips to ease his entry. Still, a whimper managed to escape her.

He immediately stopped and lifted his head, his expression taut and startled. "Am I hurting you?" His voice was gruff but still tender with concern.

She held on to his broad shoulders, feeling warmth suffuse her face under his scrutiny. "I, uh, it's been a long time...."

He stared down at her as if he wanted to ask just how long, then the question ebbed from his gaze. Josie was grateful because she didn't want to have to lie to Seth, not here, not now when they'd finally managed to put the bit-

terness of the past aside. Not when he was in the process
of claiming her so completely.

A warm, private smile brushed his mouth and he gently
ran his fingers down her cheek, a feather touch so tender it
made her breath catch. ''We'll take it slow and easy, then,''
he said in a deep drawl.

He spent the next half hour perfecting slow and easy,
using his mouth and hands until she softened and relaxed
enough to accommodate him in one smooth thrust. He slid
deeply, and their delighted moans mingled. Then the won-
drous climb began.

The final culmination was rich and breathless.

Seth groaned, burying his face in the crook of her neck.
''Josie...'' His voice was both anguished and awed.

She understood. She clung to him as the same emotions
poured through her, and something profound happened to
her in that moment. Something she was helpless to prevent
despite the foolishness of taking such a huge risk.

Her heart opened up and let Seth inside.

Sighing gruffly with total contentment, he tucked her naked body against his chest and wrapped his arms securely
around her. He nuzzled her neck and found her ear. ''I'm
gonna burn that damned flannel nightgown of yours,'' he
murmured humorously.

She smiled and cuddled closer, absorbing the heat of his
body and the gentle strength of his embrace. ''No, you
aren't,'' she argued lightly. ''It keeps me warm in the winter.''

''Not anymore,'' he said with more than a touch of male
arrogance. ''You've got me for that.''

She didn't argue, and for the first time in her life, she
found herself looking forward to cold winter nights and the
ways Seth would generate heat.

*   *   *

Sunday morning dawned bright and warm, with shafts of sunlight streaming through the bedroom window. Josie slowly rolled to her back and stretched languidly, attempting to ease her stiff muscles. She felt deliciously satiated and surprisingly rested, considering Seth had kept her up for half the night. No one could claim that they weren't well and truly wed—their marriage had been suitably consummated. Numerous times.

The man beside her didn't so much as stir, and she smiled at how incredibly handsome her husband was, how virile and sexy. As he lay deep in sleep, the hard line of his jaw had softened, and his mouth was curved in a slight smile. She longed to touch him, awaken him with a slow, familiar caress, but decided she'd rather surprise him with breakfast in bed. They had the rest of their lives to make love, and her heart fluttered at the thought.

Quietly, so as not to disturb Seth, she eased out of bed and went into the adjoining bathroom. While she was there, she brushed her teeth and ran a comb through her tangled hair. She debated whether to braid the strands, then decided not to.

Suddenly, as she gazed at her reflection, her eyes widened and her face flushed. Good Lord, she never strutted around in the nude!

Tiptoeing back into the bedroom, she picked up the first article of clothing she spied—Seth's shirt—and slipped it on. She worked on the buttons swiftly and efficiently.

"Mornin', wife."

Her pulse leaped, in surprise and in pleasure of Seth's husky greeting. *Wife*, not bride. She'd finally earned her rightful title. As silly as it seemed, something about the sentiment warmed her.

"Hi," she said, suddenly feeling shy, which was ridiculous considering the things they'd done the night before.

"What're you doin' up so early?" His voice was raspy from sleep, the provocative sound tugging at feminine senses.

He casually tucked his hands behind his head, and she couldn't help noticing that he'd nearly kicked the bedcovers off. In the light of day, his chest looked stronger, wider, more well defined. His hips were narrow, his belly lean... She followed the arrow of dark hair until it disappeared beneath the sheet.

She forced herself to glance away from that particular distraction. "I, um..." She grappled for her train of thought and miraculously found it. *What was she doing up so early?* "It's nearly 8:00 a.m." Late for them, considering that on weekdays they woke as early as 4:00 a.m.

A dark brow arched. "You gotta be somewhere today?"

She toyed with the hem of his shirt, not trusting herself to move closer to the bed. "Well, no, but I was thinking of making us some breakfast. I'm sure you're hungry."

He rolled to his side, propping himself up on his elbow. She gasped as that thin sheet slithered over his hip, uncovering a taut buttock but strategically concealing more masculine parts. "Oh, I'm plenty hungry, wife, but not for food."

The melting began, starting in the pit of her stomach and radiating outward toward her thighs. "Seth..."

"Breakfast can wait another hour. After all, we're on our honeymoon."

She laughed when she realized that his assessment was correct. They were over a month behind schedule, but they were still entitled to a few days of private indulgence. "Yes, I guess we are, aren't we?" And since Kellie wouldn't be home until that afternoon, they had the house to themselves for a few more hours.

She started toward the bed, then stopped as something

caught her eye. Sometime during the night, Seth had hung his new tan Stetson on the bedpost nearest her side of the bed, across from the other hat she'd shot off his head the day he'd come to claim her and the Golden M.

Amusement curled through her. "What's this?" she asked, spinning the hat on the post the same way Seth had done to the mangled Stetson when he'd first seen it hanging on her bedpost on their wedding day. "An addition to my collection?"

"Yep. After last night, I'd say you earned it, Josie darlin'."

A delicious heat washed through her entire body, but she couldn't stop grinning. His words, and his sweet gesture, were a wonderful compliment.

He feigned a stern look. "Now you just have to promise not to ever shoot it off my head."

She laughed, and unable to resist temptation, she plucked the Stetson from the post and put it on her head. "I'll be happy to share it. You can wear it during the day, and I can were it here, in the privacy of our bedroom."

A wolfish smile lifted his lips. "Yeah, I like the idea of having my own private cowgirl." His gaze captured hers, and in the next moment he grew serious. "I've got something else for you that you've earned."

He looked nervous, a little uncertain, and she found that touch of vulnerability in Seth endearing. "Oh? Was I that good last night?"

"Better than good." Still lying in bed with that sheet barely covering him, he nodded toward the dresser they shared. "It's in the top drawer, left-hand side."

Curious, she rummaged past his folded briefs and socks until she discovered a small black velvet box tucked away in the corner. Heart pounding, she retrieved the gift and turned to face him. "What's this?"

He didn't move, his entire body seemingly taut with an anxious kind of energy. "Open it and see."

She moved to the bed to be near him. Tentatively, she started to open the lid, then gasped when she'd unveiled a beautiful diamond ring surrounded by bright, fiery emeralds. It was gorgeous, and judging by the size of the single diamond and the dozen or so emeralds around it, the piece of jewelry had to have cost him a small fortune.

Unable to speak and mouth still gaping in shock, she lifted her gaze to his.

He sat up, and with the sheet still tangled around his hips, he clasped her left hand. "I know it's not your traditional bridal set, but the emeralds match your eyes, and I couldn't resist."

Tender, hopeful emotions crowded her chest as he slipped the sparkling ring onto the appropriate finger, claiming her as his. Nothing had ever felt so perfect. So right.

He looked up at her, and she lost herself in his smoky blue eyes and gorgeous smile. "I was waiting for the right time to give you the ring. No better time than the night after making you my wife."

The significance of his gesture wasn't lost on her. She was well and truly his wife. Bound and committed to him forever, as he was to her.

"It's…too much," her more practical side couldn't help but protest. She might have expected a simple gold band, but he'd obviously spared no expense. "Certainly more than I need and more money than you ought to have spent."

Reaching up, he tugged playfully on the brim of his hat. "Worrying about money should be the least of your concerns, Josie."

She could feel a frown forming on her brow because she

couldn't help but wonder if Seth had frivolous spending habits she didn't know about. She'd spent years trying to thwart her father's carefree ways with money. Did she have to worry about Seth's squandering money needlessly, too?

He seemed to have read her mind, and addressed her concern. "I'm a saver by nature, honey, but when I buy things, I buy the best. Since I didn't have anything to spend my paycheck from the Paradise Wild on, I've accumulated quite a fat bank account. The money is ours, to use as we like or as we need."

She didn't want to rely on him and his money, but she knew in his own way he was making this marriage an equal union. What belonged to him now was hers, as well. He was trusting her with everything he possessed.

It made her deception all the more troublesome and disturbing, but she wasn't sure she was ready to share her own secrets just yet. Wasn't sure he'd accept the truth when he'd always believed the worst. And, ultimately, the thought of his rejection after they'd finally established a fragile truce made her shudder inwardly.

"You're thinking too much, wife," he said, and rolling to his back, he finally tossed off the covers, thoroughly scattering her troubling thoughts and replacing them with the thrill of anticipation and need. He crooked a finger at her, wicked intent in his gaze. "C'mere, cowgirl," he cajoled sexily.

Shaking off her unease, she went to her husband, unable to deny him anything. It didn't take long for the languid slide of his hands to soothe her uncertainties, and the warmth of his mouth to replace her fears with an all-consuming passion.

CHAPTER TEN

THE time had come for truths, Seth decided, because guilt was clashing with his growing feelings for Josie. He intended, once and for all, to absolve himself of the cruel lies he'd inflicted on Josie eleven years ago. Lies that still stood between them and preyed on his conscience. Lies that impeded a deeper, emotional level of intimacy in their marriage.

Leaning against the porch railing in the dark, Seth gazed out at the expanse of stars scattered in the night sky, mulling over the different ways to address the sensitive subject.

It had been a week and a half since Josie had so willingly given herself to him, and with every day that passed, Seth was beginning to realize how much he cared for Josie. Despite all reason and a past filled with resentment and bitterness, he was falling hard for his beautiful, stubborn, spirited wife.

What had happened eleven years ago was an issue that hung over their marriage like a dark cloud, threatening the tenuous treaty they'd forged. Neither one of them spoke of the past, but that was part of the problem, he'd decided. Until they resolved all the grievances still buried beneath a veneer of civility, their marriage would never grow stronger. And he wanted more than a marriage of convenience with Josie.

He wanted a real home and a family. Her, him, Kellie, and maybe a few babies of their own. The thought filled him with warmth and a contentment he hadn't recognized was missing from his life until that moment.

He was willing to confess his youthful wrongdoing of eleven years ago. Hopefully, in turn, Josie would extend the same faith in him and they could put that part of their lives behind them and look toward the future, which wouldn't include any grudges from the past.

Both he and Josie had grown and changed over the years. No longer did he view Josie as the scheming girl he'd thought she once was. The weeks since their marriage had shown him a strong, independent woman who'd struggled with running a ranch, raising a daughter alone and attempting to foil her father's destructive gambling habits. A woman with an enormous amount of pride, a mulish streak a country-mile wide and a heart that embraced her family.

He wanted that heart to embrace him.

The creaking of the screen door brought Seth out of his reverie. He glanced over his shoulder just as Josie stepped from the house and onto the porch. She was wearing a soft lavender summer dress and sandals, and the curly ends of her unbound hair shimmered in the light filtering out from the foyer. Her face glowed with femininity, and something much sweeter. Love? he wondered.

She slipped behind him and wrapped her arms around his middle, tucked her thumbs into the waistband of his jeans just above his belt buckle and pressed her body against his. He felt the crush of her supple breasts along his spine, the slide of her thighs along the back of his, and his belly grew taut.

She rose on tiptoe and nipped lightly at his earlobe. "What are you doing out here all alone?"

"Just thinking," he said, enjoying her sensual play. Since making love, she'd grown bold and uninhibited, more times than not initiating caresses and kisses of her own. He was reaping the rewards of an insatiable, incredibly sexy wife.

Her palms slid over the muscular ridges of his stomach and up to the hard plane of his chest. "About what?" she murmured.

A groan of pleasure rolled up into his throat, and he managed to swallow it. "You, and me."

"Hmmm." She found his nipple through his cotton shirt and toyed with the hardened nub. "Sounds serious."

Serious enough that he didn't want Kellie to overhear their conversation. Serious enough that he didn't want to be distracted by the lure of her touches and the promise of where those soft, stroking hands could lead to.

He turned around, breaking the contact of their bodies, and held his hand out to her. "Take a walk with me?"

"Sure." A vixen smile curled her mouth, and she trustingly folded her hand in his, following him down the steps and across the lawn toward the stables. Hugging his side, she said in a low, sultry voice, "What do you say we sneak into the barn, climb up to the loft, and I'll show you the moon and stars from the window there?"

He didn't doubt that his feisty wife would show him the moon and stars and take him to heaven while she was at it. While the idea of whisking her away for a lovers' tryst was a welcome way to spend the next hour or two, he wasn't about to let the temptation deter him from tonight's mission. "Maybe later?"

A slight frown creased her brow, as if she couldn't quite believe he'd refuse such an invitation. "Okay," she said softly.

He veered toward the fence bordering the pasture, moonlight guiding the way. Crickets chirped a serenade, along with other night insects. The whinny of horses in the nearby corrals added to the cacophony.

The familiar sounds should have relaxed Seth, but they did nothing to ease the apprehension swirling in his belly. He had no idea how this long-overdue conversation might turn out, or how Josie would react to his admission. Just because she'd used him for her own means didn't make the lie he'd fabricated to hurt her any less malicious or devastating.

So why couldn't he shake the unease curling through him? Because, he realized, he was actually nervous about the outcome. A part of him feared losing Josie all over again.

And that's when he knew he was in love with her.

Coming to an abrupt halt, he plowed all ten of his fingers into her lush curls, cupped the back of her head and brought her mouth up to his for a soul-searing kiss. She returned the embrace, sliding her arms around his neck and offering herself so freely, so sweetly, to him. His heart thundered behind his ribs, his emotions crashing on a wave of sentiment so powerful, he was helpless to resist its allure.

He loved her. Had he ever stopped? At that moment, he didn't think so. She was the only woman he'd ever craved, even when he fought to forget her.

He kissed her fiercely, hungrily, desperately, and she accepted his sensual assault, returning it with her own brand of desire. So much passion. So much need. It nearly consumed him.

When he finally lifted his head, Josie looked up at him with a dazed expression, yet one clouded with concern. "Seth..." Her voice was breathless. "What's wrong?"

He pulled in a deep breath that had no effect on his rapidly beating pulse, nor did it ease the ache in his heart. "I'd like to talk to you."

She dragged her tongue along her bottom lip, moonlight illuminating the uncertainty in her gaze. "All right."

His hands were still tangled in her hair, and he lowered one of them so he could skim his thumb along her soft cheek. "About what happened between us eleven years ago."

If he'd meant to put a damper on the tender moment, his request certainly managed to do it. She visibly recoiled, her entire body tensing. Grasping his wrists, Josie removed his hands from her face and stepped away. "I don't think that's such a good idea."

He didn't like the way she was retreating, seemingly hiding from an issue that needed to be confronted. "Why not?"

Crossing her hands over her chest, she rubbed her bare arms as if chilled, though the night was pleasantly warm. "Because nothing will change what happened in the past, and I think resurrecting those old memories will only create more problems, rather than resolve anything."

He strongly disagreed. "Don't you think we need to discuss those memories rationally before we can leave them behind?"

"Not necessarily," she said, then sighed deeply. "It's a part of our past, Seth. Neither one of us will ever forget that."

"Forget, no," he agreed. "But what about forgiving?"

"I forgive you for being such a jerk."

He stared at her, his mouth twisting ruefully. He couldn't tell by her expressionless features if she was joking or not, but he didn't like being solely implicated for an offense that had been shared. "How gracious of you," he said, his tone faintly sarcastic. "But there's more to it than that. It works both ways, Josie. I need to forgive you, as well."

"What for?" There was no mistaking the rising irritation in her voice or the defensive straightening of her back. "You're the one who used me for your own personal vengeance against a McAllister!"

"And you slept with me, then tried to pass your unborn child off as mine," he retorted just as heatedly.

An incredulous sound escaped her. "And you don't think that's at all possible?"

Her question threw him for a loop and he shook his head. Had he lost the thread of conversation somewhere? "I don't think what's possible?"

Her mouth pursed. "That the child might be yours?"

It was his turn to snort disbelievingly. "*We* used protection every time!"

She said nothing, but even in the moonlight he could see
the flare of emotion sparking in her gaze. Despair tumbled
into hurt, which gradually heated to the blaze of fury. Then
she jutted her chin out, reminding him of the obstinate,
tough woman who'd greeted him with a rifle not so long
ago.

Seth blew out a harsh breath and scrubbed a hand over
his face. Their discussion had totally taken a turn for the
worse, and he struggled to get it back on track. "Josie...this
isn't how I meant for our talk to go." Wanting to make
amends, he reached for her, intending to pull her into his
arms where she belonged.

She stepped back just as he was about to touch her, the
sudden gesture as effective as if she'd slapped his hand
away. "Then you shouldn't make accusations that you
can't prove."

"Accusations?" What the hell did she mean by that?

"You accused me of sleeping around, didn't you?"

He jammed his hands on his hips. "I didn't accuse you.
It was a—"

"A rumor?" she supplied waspishly.

He clenched his jaw. She was twisting his words around
and confusing him—and the issue! "If that's the way you
want to label it."

"Tell me, then, how would *you* label it?" she asked, her
acid tone provoking him. "Rumors? Hearsay? Locker-room
gossip?"

If she had a point, he felt as though he was missing it
by a mile, and that fact made him as surly as a provoked
bear. "What difference does it make?" he roared, frustration riding him hard. "I don't understand what you're getting so damned worked up about!"

"No, I guess you wouldn't." Her voice was calm, but
the emotions he saw in her eyes were as turbulent as a
storm-swept sea. "A woman's reputation is more easily
destroyed by a few simple victory claims than a man's."

"I'm sorry that your reputation was ruined," he said, forcing a placidity he was far from feeling. "But *I* didn't do it!"

"Of course you didn't. You were too intent on pursuing your own brand of revenge." Bristling with anger, she brushed past him toward the house.

He swore helplessly under his breath; the entire situation seemed to be unraveling before him. "It was a lie," he called after her.

That stopped her retreat, and she slowly turned around, her gaze intent on him. "Excuse me?"

Since he had her undivided attention, he decided to go for broke. He had nothing left to lose at this point in their conversation. "I lied to you." When she just stared at him as if she didn't understand, he continued. "I fell hard for you back then, Josie. I never lied about my feelings for you. When you told me you were pregnant, I was going to marry you even though I was scared of what my father would do to me." Closing his eyes, he pinched the bridge of his nose with his fingers, remembering confiding in Jay and what his brother had told him. He hadn't believed Jay's claim at first... He glanced at Josie, who was still standing there, waiting for more. "Then I heard that you'd slept with other guys, and I was furious. Guys I knew were talking about scoring with you! Your baby wasn't mine. That's when I lost it and told you that I'd slept with you out of revenge. I only wanted to hurt you as much as you hurt me."

Moisture glittered in her eyes, combining moonlight and more brittle emotions. "That certainly did the trick."

He was beginning to feel like the sole bad guy in this scenario and he didn't like it one bit. "What did you expect, Josie?"

"I don't know," she said quietly, and swallowed back what he suspected was a rush of tears. "But I certainly can't compete with the rumors. I never could, and it seems I never will be able to.''

She turned again to walk away, but pride and fury collided in Seth, and he acted upon them. Grabbing her arm, he spun her around, guessing by her sharp gasp and the widening of her eyes that his expression was as dark and thunderous as his mood.

''What are you talking about?'' he demanded through gritted teeth.

''They were rumors, Seth!'' she yelled at him.

He scowled darkly at her. How could she claim what he'd heard with his own ears as rumors? He'd heard the allegations, the bragging, and they had made him sick. And now she was claiming they weren't true? Did she think he was that stupid that she could dupe him all over again with more lies?

She was spitting mad, furious, and it showed in the way she struggled out of his grasp. He was stronger and wasn't about to let go just yet.

''*I'm* trying to be honest here.'' His low voice vibrated with barely suppressed hostility.

''So am I,'' she fumed, and tossed her head back. ''It's awfully noble of you to assuage your guilt about your revenge scheme, but I have absolutely *nothing* to feel guilty about!''

''Josie...'' His tone reverberated with a dangerous warning.

She chose to ignore it. ''Let go of me, Seth.'' Tears welled in her eyes, and he realized how close she was to falling apart on him. But with a mutinous lift of her chin, she became as formidable as she'd been with a rifle. ''In fact, I'd appreciate it if you didn't touch me at all.''

Her insinuation was unmistakable, and he released her. After less than two weeks of wedded bliss, they were back to being angry adversaries.

* * *

Josie turned onto her side on the narrow bed in the guest bedroom and drew the extra pillow to her chest, hugging it tightly in an attempt to keep herself from falling apart. Physically, the soft cushion did the trick and kept her body from trembling too badly. Emotionally, a mere pillow wasn't much of a support when everything within her was fragmenting into a million pieces.

Seth didn't believe her. He hadn't said those exact words, but she didn't need a verbal confirmation to validate the disbelief she'd seen glaring in his eyes. And in that moment, she hated him for breaking the fragile heart that had grown to love him again.

She'd all but screamed the truth in his face, offering him her most treasured secret for him to grasp, presenting him with the opportunity to realize that what was hers also belonged to him. Instead, he'd opted to believe the worst, that she'd been unscrupulous during their brief affair eleven years ago. He believed the rumors and gossip, and there was nothing left that she could say or do to change Seth's low opinion of her. The knowledge that her husband would always harbor some kind of resentment toward her hurt way down deep inside. It was the same misery she'd kept tucked away for eleven long, lonely years.

He'd lied. His admission brought her little comfort, considering how long she'd lived with the pain of believing he'd used her for his own personal revenge on a McAllister, then tossed her aside when she'd needed him the most. She decided she wouldn't try to defend herself or deny once more the false claims that had ruined her life. She had absolutely nothing to prove to the man she'd been forced to marry.

And that, she realized, was the crux of it all. If it hadn't been for the Golden M, Seth never would have given her a second glance. He didn't want a wife, but he'd been saddled with one anyway. He didn't want *her*, but he was bound to her by the marriage vows they'd both spoken.

They would be together til death them did part, or divorce forced one of them out.

Both of them wanted the Golden M too much to give it up so easily to the other. That thought brought on a spurt of anger. Dammit, this was *her* home, not his! If her father hadn't so foolishly gambled away the Golden M, she could have been spared this awful degradation Seth was putting her through!

A quick, rapping knock on the door made her heart kick against her ribs. She didn't respond, didn't say anything, knowing this late at night it was Seth, not Kellie, who'd come to seek her out. She'd been waiting for him to come back to the main house and discover that she was no longer going to play the submissive wife to his barbarian demands.

"Josie?" he called in a low voice so as not to wake Kellie, who slept in the next room.

She huddled deeper under the covers and didn't answer, hoping he'd take the hint and leave.

She heard him sigh. A deep, heavy release of breath. "You're a light sleeper and I know you're awake. I want you to come back to our room."

Oh, she just bet he did, the arrogant boar! "No." Too late, she realized she'd broken the silence, therefore inviting him to respond.

The knob turned, but the door didn't open. She reveled in a moment of satisfaction; she'd secured the lock before climbing into bed.

"You can't sleep in there forever." Frustration edged his voice.

"Don't bet the ranch on that, cowboy," she said smugly. "You'd lose. This bed is just the right size for *one*."

"Josie, you're being irrational."

"*I'm* being irrational?" Finding it difficult to be appropriately huffy and indignant lying down, she sat upright in bed and tossed off the covers, glaring at the closed door. "What does that make you? After all but branding me a whore this evening for something you *heard* eleven years ago, you still want me in your bed. How rational is that?''

"I *never* said you were a...a whore!''

"It was what you *didn't* say.''

She heard a soft *thunk* and guessed he was resting his forehead against the wooden door. "Josie, we had a disagreement. All married couples argue. It's normal, and we can't resolve things if you shut me out.''

It had been a far more personal issue than a disagreement, not that she'd ever expect him to understand how deeply her pain ran. "According to you, there's nothing to resolve.'' He was right, and she was wrong.

"Dammit, Josie!'' he growled in exasperation. "You belong in our bed!''

"Whatever for?'' She affected her sweetest voice just to annoy him even more. "Our marriage is consummated, my duty is done, and my half of the ranch is secure, so there's no need for any further intimate relations between us.''

"You're my *wife*,'' he bit out irritably.

She squeezed her eyes shut, refusing to give in to the prickling sensation behind her eyes. *She would not cry over Seth O'Connor!* "You've got yourself a business partner, Seth, not a wife,'' she said flatly. "That's the way it should have been from the beginning.''

"Josie, please...'' A desperate quality touched his voice.

Feeling tired and weary, she sank back onto the mattress. "Go away and leave me alone.''

He must have realized he'd lost that round because she heard him stomp away, cursing under his breath.

Josie just felt lost, period. At the rate she and Seth were going, it was very likely the feud between their families would never end.

Seth slid from Lexi's saddle, untied the knapsack that held his midday meal and tossed the reins aside so the horse could graze while he took his break. He headed to a shady tree away from the rest of his men, who'd opted for a cooler spot near the creek. Seth glared at Mac as he approached on his own mare and wondered what the foreman wanted. Couldn't the old man see that he wasn't in the mood for company and he was intruding on his brooding time?

From atop his horse, Mac eyed him with an annoying combination of amusement and concern. "You okay, boss?"

"I'm fine," Seth snapped, taking out of his knapsack the same boring lunch he'd packed himself for the past week. Two bologna and cheese sandwiches, a can of juice and an apple. Josie had informed him a business partner wasn't responsible for his meals and he was on his own. He scowled at Mac as if his bland lunch was all his fault. "And why do you keep asking me if I'm okay?"

Mac smothered a grin. "Because you've been barking orders at everyone for the past five days. The men are just about ready to hog-tie you and leave you out on the range for the buzzards to pick at. But before they did that, I told them I'd come on over and see if I couldn't remove that burr you got stuck under your saddle."

"Don't waste your time, old man." Josie wasn't your ordinary burr.

As was typical of Mac, Seth's words had no effect on him. The foreman dismounted, grabbed his own lunch and joined Seth beneath the tree. He began unpacking his meal, bringing out a barbecued chicken sandwich, potato salad and a bowl of fresh mixed fruit. Seth's mouth watered, and his appetite for his own lunch waned.

Mac ate half of his barbecued chicken before finally breaking the silence with his own opinion on the matter. "I'm guessing your problem is with Josie."

Seth forced himself to take a bite of greasy bologna and processed cheese. "That woman is nothing but a thorn in my side."

"Want to talk about it?"

"No." What he wanted was Mac's lunch. "She's stubborn and pigheaded, and I'm just about at my wit's end with her. She blows everything I say out of proportion, puts words in my mouth, generally hates my guts and is making my life miserable. Maybe I ought to just give her the divorce she wants." He tossed his half-eaten sandwich onto his knapsack in disgust. So much for not wanting to talk about his problems with Josie.

"You'd give up that easily?" Mac asked neutrally.

"It's what she wants." Grabbing his can of juice, he popped the top and chugged the warm liquid down in one long swallow.

"You sure about that?"

Seth caught the delicious scent of homemade potato salad and his stomach growled demandingly. "She'd be the first in line to wave goodbye as I headed out the door."

Mac's easy grin reached his eyes. "She'd miss you."

Seth's answer was a disbelieving snort. Bracing his back against the tree trunk, he lowered his Stetson over his eyes, dismissing the foreman and their discussion with the intention of a quick nap.

"You obviously don't see the way the girl looks at you." Mac rudely ignored his attempt to rest peacefully. "She's heartsick over you."

"You're crazy, old man," he muttered. If Josie was heartsick, then she had a helluva way of showing it with her brassy, I-don't-give-a-damn attitude.

"All this sun does tend to take its toll," Mac agreed to the possibility of being mentally unbalanced. "But I've known Josie her entire life, and there's only one other time when she's looked the way she does now."

"Please enlighten me," Seth drawled wryly from beneath the brim of his hat. "And tell me when that was."

"When the two of you broke things off the first time all those years ago."

Everything in Seth tensed. Slowly, he tipped his hat back

and narrowed his gaze on Mac. The man knew entirely too much for his own good. "What happened eleven years ago is different from now."

Mac frowned as if the point eluded him. "You had a fight, didn't you?"

"Yes." Frustration steamed in Seth when he recalled his argument with Josie. A wave of anger prompted him to blurt out, "She's holding things against me that I have no control over!"

Mac savored a succulent slice of peach before asking, "Such as?"

"Rumors," Seth said, summing up the situation with the word Josie had used repeatedly. "About her."

"Ahh," Mac said as if he totally comprehended the situation.

Thing was, Seth had the strangest feeling that the wily old man *did* understand.

There was silence as Mac leisurely ate a juicy wedge of watermelon. His stomach growling more fiercely than before, Seth rummaged through his knapsack for his own fruit and bit a chunk from his apple. It was dry compared to Mac's fresh selection of fruit.

"You know, I never was one to believe rumors," Mac said, finally breaking the quiet spell between them.

"I heard the *facts* with my own ears." He'd told Josie the same thing, but that detail hadn't seemed to matter to her.

"What kind of facts?"

Seth chose his words carefully, not wanting to be crude or offend Mac. "That Josie was, well, promiscuous, and I was just an added fling. A father to claim for her unborn child."

A thoughtful look flickered across Mac's weathered face as he finished off his fruit. He packed away the remains of his lunch, stretched out on his side on the soft grass and regarded Seth curiously. "Every wonder who might be at the source of such nastiness?"

Seth's brows snapped together. "What do you mean?"

Mac slowly shook his head. "For someone who's so smart, you sure don't know much about women."

Feeling appropriately insulted, Seth clenched his jaw in indignation. "Get to the point, old man, and fast."

"First, no matter what you believe, I've never known Josie to be…what's that big word again?"

"Promiscuous," Seth supplied, his patience quickly dwindling.

"Yeah, that," Mac said, waving his hand between them as if he had no use for such fancy vocabulary. "Don't you think behavior like that would continue? We both know women who like to cat around, and they've always been that way. It's a part of who they are. Don't you think it's a tad odd that Josie didn't become a loose woman over the years?"

Unexpectedly, Seth's stomach clenched. He'd never analyzed the situation quite that way, but then, anger, and a tremendous blow to his ego, had driven him eleven years ago. Now he was able to examine the situation as a rational, twenty-nine-year-old man and not the hotheaded eighteen-year-old he'd once been.

"Yeah, I guess I see your point," Seth admitted, though he still felt as though something was missing from the equation. Something just beyond his grasp but there nonetheless.

Plucking a long blade of grass, Mac chewed on the end. "So, who would have the most to gain by starting the rumors?"

They were back to *rumors* again. Sighing, he brought up his jean-clad knee, draped a wrist across the top and straightened his other leg. "They weren't exactly rumors," he tried to explain. "I heard guys I knew in school bragging about Josie. Isn't that pretty much hearing it from the horse's mouth?''

Mac shrugged. ''Depends on whether or not the horse had been paid to neigh certain things that might hurt one person and anger another.''

Adrenaline speeded up Seth's pulse as he thought about the possibility of such a scheme. And then he shook off the notion. ''This is crazy,'' he said, unable to believe someone could be that desperate. ''Who would want to hurt Josie badly enough that they'd pay to destroy her reputation...?''

Seth's blood heated as the past rushed in on him, important bits and pieces that forced him to reevaluate what had happened a lifetime ago.

His brother had been the first to learn of Josie's pregnancy. Instead of the support he expected, Seth had been dealt a staggering blow.

How do you know it's your baby? His brother had asked him. *Considering she's slept with half the senior class, there's no telling whose brat it is.*

Then the allegations had started. Rumors he'd believed. Rumors that made him vindictive and blind to the truth. Rumors that made sure he'd have nothing to do with a McAllister.

There was only one person he knew who hated Josie McAllister enough to destroy the love he and Josie had once shared.

Jay.

White-hot fury ripped through him, and he jumped to his feet and jabbed an accusatory finger at Mac. ''You've known all along!''

''I've suspected,'' Mac said with a casual lift of his shoulders. ''Josie just isn't the kind of girl to be...whatever that fancy word is. She never has been and never will be.''

It was that simple...and still so complicated. Good God, for how many years had he believed the worst, hating Josie for an offense she'd never committed? The same amount of years she'd lived with the pain of his rejection and complete loathing. The same amount of years she'd raised a daughter that was also his.

He felt physically ill. It was no wonder she despised him.

He strode toward his horse, determination and rage fueling him.

"Where you off to, boss?" Mac asked easily, as if he hadn't just turned his entire world upside down.

Seth swung up into the saddle in one lithe movement and reached for Lexi's reins. As much as his instincts urged him to race home to talk to Josie and look at Kellie and see her as his own daughter for the first time, he had to rid himself of the awful anger and bitterness welling inside him before he could reconcile with his new family.

Meeting Mac's gaze, he gave him a slight nod, silently thanking him for his wisdom and intervention. "Seems to me I've got a score to settle with my brother."

CHAPTER ELEVEN

SETH barged into his brother's office on the Paradise Wild without knocking. Jay glanced up, startled at the intrusion, but Seth didn't give him a chance to speak. Bracing his hands on the desk that separated them, Seth leaned across the surface, looked his brother straight in the eye and said in a venomously low voice, "Depending how generous I feel after I hear a few things from you, I might let you live."

Jay quickly recovered his composure, covering up his stunned expression with a smirk. "Married life certainly doesn't agree with you. Is your wife not as accommodating as you'd hoped she'd be?"

Rage gripped him, and he struggled to keep his temper from exploding. "If you ever say another derogatory thing about my wife, it'll be your last." His tone was chilling and dangerous.

Jay met his stare defiantly but thought better of further provoking him. "So, then, to what do I owe the pleasure of your visit?"

"I want some straight answers from you."

"About what?"

"About Josie, and the guys she supposedly slept with."

Trepidation flashed in Jay's eyes, then he shrugged in casual disregard. "What would I know about that?"

Seth resisted the savage urge to reach across the desk, grab Jay by the collar and shake the truth from him. "Think back and try real hard to remember whom you bribed to spread those malicious rumors."

His brother began shuffling papers on his desk, giving

the task more attention than it warranted. "I don't know what you're talking about."

"Oh, I think you do." Seth straightened, every muscle in his body coiled tight. "You paid a handful of guys in my senior class to brag about being with Josie so I'd hear them, and believe the lies."

"What you're suggesting is ridiculous," Jay scoffed, a nervous tremor in his voice.

"Were you, or were you not, the source of those rumors?" Seth asked with deadly calm.

Jay glanced up, his lips thinning. And then, as if realizing he was backed into a tight corner, he scrambled for a way to fight his way out. "Josie was just using you, and you were too blind to see that!"

It wasn't the confession Seth was looking for. "It's a simple question, brother. Yes, or no?"

"She was going to trap you into marriage!" Jay blurted, his voice tinged with desperation.

"Answer me!" Seth bellowed, slamming a fist down on the desk.

Jay abruptly stood, sending his chair crashing into the wall behind him. "Yes!" His blatant answer seemed to surprise him, but once he'd said it, he jutted his chin out belligerently. "I did it! And it accomplished exactly what it needed to."

A muscle in Seth's jaw ticked. "Which was?"

"It was the only way to protect you from that tra…from *her*! McAllisters don't know anything but how to lie, cheat and steal! And they always have ulterior motives! If you married her, she would've tried to get her hands on our land."

Seth found it hard to believe his brother could think such a thing of Josie. She was one of the most honest, hard-working women he knew. "So, you took it upon yourself to destroy Josie's reputation and make us hate one another?'' Seth slowly started around the desk toward his brother until he was towering over him.

Jay stood his ground. "It worked."

"I lost ten years with my daughter!" he roared, the anguish of that statement seemingly ripping from his soul. "Ten years that I can never get back! You have kids of your own. Doesn't that mean anything to you?"

"She's a McAllister," he spit out.

"She's got O'Connor blood running through her veins," Seth said through gritted teeth. "*My* blood!"

Jay said nothing, just glared.

Seth shook his head in disgust. "God, you're just as spiteful as our father was." Deciding he'd had enough, Seth turned to go.

"At least I'm not a traitor," Jay sneered.

The slight was more than Seth could take, and everything he'd endured over the past eleven years came to a boiling head. Jay's betrayal. His father's bitterness that had cost him half of Paradise Wild. Losing Josie and missing the chance to know the beautiful, sweet girl who was his daughter.

Whirling back around, he grabbed a handful of Jay's shirt and slammed him into the wall hard enough to hear his teeth rattle. Jay's stunned expression quickly evaporated as survival instincts kicked in. Jay threw the first punch, clipping Seth along the jaw. That was the only invitation Seth needed to reciprocate.

They hadn't fought with their fists since they were teenagers, but the battle was long overdue. They both took their anger and years of accumulated bitterness out on the other. Fists flew, connecting with bone and muscle. Grunts of fury and pain filled the office, along with vicious curses and an occasional taunt.

Papers on the desk scattered as a hand reached out to break a fall. A filing cabinet toppled over from the strength of a male body rushing it. Pictures on the wall crashed to the floor and furniture was overturned. And then they were on the ground, rolling around and throwing punches as the opportunity presented itself. Though Seth was larger, Jay was a worthy opponent and managed his share of damage.

"Stop!" a hysterical voice screamed from behind them. "You're going to kill each other!"

Seth recognized the voice as belonging to his sister-in-law. "I'm working on it!" he said in between panting breaths, then grunted as Jay took advantage of the distraction and planted a fist in his belly, bringing him to his knees.

With a low growl, Seth lunged, tackling Jay. Jay groaned as he cracked his head against the floor, then blinked as if seeing stars. Seth came up on his knees and leaned over Jay just as a merciless smile curled his brother's lip and he threw a punch, albeit a weak one, that connected with the corner of Seth's eye.

Ignoring the burning pain, Seth pounced on Jay as he struggled to stand up, and just when he was about to return the black eye, they were both doused with cold water. Sucking in a breath at the unexpected shower, they jumped apart. Seth scowled at the woman responsible for the diversion.

Erin stood feet away from them, an empty metal bucket in her hand, her expression furious. "Sorry to ruin your fun, boys, but that's enough!" Her fiery gaze encompassed them both. "What do you two think you're doing?"

"Having it out?" Seth offered as water dripped off his nose and chin.

She didn't find his attempt at levity the least bit humorous. "You're acting like hormonal teenagers! You guys are all the family you have left. This has to stop!"

Seth and Jay glared at one another, each expecting an apology from the other. The silence grew thick.

Finally, Seth turned toward Erin. "Nothing I say or do will get through to him. He's intent on hating me for mar-

rying Josie, and he's punishing Josie for a seventy-five-
year-old feud that she's not responsible for.'' Swiping at
the cut on his bottom lip with the back of his hand, he
glanced at Jay again. ''I love you because you're my
brother. But I love my wife and daughter more. Until you
can be civil with me and my family, consider me in the
enemy camp.''

Jay digested that, and Seth thought he saw a glimmer of
possibility in his hazel eyes. As though he was grappling
with the longing to forge a truce but still being tangled up
in the bitterness and resentment their father had instilled so
deeply into him.

Regret wove through Seth and he gave Erin a curt nod.
''Now if you'll excuse me, I have a more important matter
to tend to.''

The man who stumbled into the kitchen looked like he'd
been in a barroom brawl. Kellie gasped in shock, and
Josie's stomach gave an odd twist as she took in Seth's
split lip, the purplish red discoloration around the corner of
his left eye, and a nasty scrape on his jaw.

''Seth, what happened?'' Forgetting that she was angry
enough with her husband to spit nails, she stopped chop-
ping the vegetables she and Kellie were preparing for dinner and went to him.

And stopped halfway there.

His gaze was focused on Kellie, intense and searching,
the depths of his blue eyes filled with a personal anguish
that made Josie's breath catch.

He knew. She didn't know how he'd learned the truth,
but somehow he knew the secret she'd protected for eleven
long years. But did he believe it, or were the lies about her
still clouding his ability to accept the truth that was staring
back at him with wide, trusting green eyes?

''Where have you been?'' she asked, hating the trembling quality of her voice.

Finally, he shifted his gaze to her, which now encompassed a wealth of regret and guilt. "I was defending a woman's honor and settling a few scores with my brother. Now I'd like to settle a few things with you."

Dread churned within her, and she steeled herself to defend her position, and her daughter, if need be. Not wanting Kellie to be privy to their conversation until she knew what Seth had to say, she turned to the young girl, who still stood by the sink, looking uncertain and more than a little shaken by Seth's roughed-up appearance.

"Honey, Seth and I need a little time alone," Josie said, careful to keep her voice calm. "Maybe you could go upstairs and find me some antiseptic, bandages and cotton balls so I can get Seth cleaned up."

"Okay," she said, and skirted her way around the adults and out of the room.

Seth watched Kellie leave the kitchen, then flicked his gaze back to Josie, who was nervously twisting her hands together in front of her. Defiance sparked from her beautiful green eyes, but he wasn't here to condemn, just to uncover the truth.

"She's mine, isn't she?" he asked, shattering the silence between them with his startling question.

Her chin rising rebelliously, Josie looked for all the world like she was preparing for a fight she planned to win. "She's *my* daughter."

Her eyes were filled with caution. She expected him to be furious for keeping Kellie a secret, he realized. But how could he summon such an angry emotion when he had to shoulder most of the blame for the way things had turned out? "She's *ours*. Can you deny that?"

She wanted to. He could see the conflicting answers in her gaze and he was curious to see which one she'd go with. She closed her eyes, a shudder visibly shaking her. Then her lashes lifted, and he saw her defeat and knew the time for truth and healing had begun. "No."

That one word nearly brought him to his knees. "Why didn't you tell me, Josie?" he asked, taking a step toward her.

Her expression wary, she backed up, establishing boundaries that didn't include his being within touching distance. "Would you have believed me?"

"You didn't even try to defend your reputation." He clearly recalled how devastated she'd been when he announced that he'd used her for revenge on a McAllister, and he'd felt sick to his stomach for doling out his own share of lies and cruelty. Yet, not once had she denied the rumors, just let him think the worst.

She gripped the counter behind her with both hands. "Would you have believed me?" she asked again, forcing him to acknowledge the question, if only internally.

No. The admission was tough to swallow, and a wave of frustration gripped him. "Goddammit, Josie, you should have told me the baby was mine!" He advanced once again, invading her personal space.

"I did!" she shouted, the gut-wrenching emotion in her raised voice bringing him to an abrupt halt. "*But you didn't believe me!*"

And that was the worst of it, Seth realized, facing what he'd denied for too long. He wanted to tell her that she should have been more adamant, tried harder to make him understand, which was foolish because he knew in his heart that her pleas wouldn't have made much difference back then. All the signs of her honesty had been there, and he'd chosen to ignore the truth instead of giving her claim the consideration it deserved.

"They were lies, Seth," she said, imploring him to understand. "I don't know how or why someone would spread such awful rumors—"

"My brother did it." He ignored her stunned catch of breath and the questions that instantly leaped to life in her gaze, and continued on before they got sidetracked. In a few minutes, he'd explain. "I was a fool to believe the lies, and they made me mad enough to retaliate, which is exactly what my brother wanted. I have no excuses because what I did was unconscionable." He swallowed the thick lump of pride lodged in his throat. "Can you forgive me?"

She gave her head a quick shake, and his hopes plummeted. "It's not as easy as that."

"It can be." It was time to up the stakes, he decided, because he couldn't bear the thought of losing this woman he'd lost once before. She was a part of him, heart and soul. "I love you, Josie McAllister O'Connor."

His heartfelt declaration didn't have the effect he was striving or hoping for. She didn't soften or rush into his arms but instead laughed humorlessly. "That's just it. I'm a McAllister. I always will be. And I'll always be the great-granddaughter of the man your family believes cheated to get this parcel of O'Connor land."

That had been his father and brother's belief, not necessarily his. "What happened all those years ago between our great-grandparents has absolutely nothing to do with us in the present. We're not responsible for their actions. We're just living the legend that's been handed down to us through the generations and doing our best to deal with the circumstances of that long-ago poker game." And then, because he couldn't stand the distance separating them, he closed the gap in three steps and ran a callused finger along the curve of her jaw. "And just to set the record straight, Josie darlin', your last name never made a bit of difference to me. Not eleven years ago, and certainly not now."

Her stiff shoulders relaxed. "You lost so much because of your involvement with me."

"None of that matters," he said, meaning it.

"How can it not?" she argued, her moist gaze searching his. "Half of Paradise Wild should have been yours, and you lost it because of *me*. Surely you have to feel some resentment over that."

A lopsided smile curved his mouth. "You would think so, but I don't. I always blamed myself, but never you directly. It was my choice to be with you eleven years ago. And my father's bitterness wasn't your fault. He was just looking for someone to blame for the fact that his grandfather lost a good chunk of land that would have been his." Tenderly, he drew her into his embrace. His optimism was bolstered when she didn't resist his caring, supportive advance. "I have exactly what I want, right here in my arms and beneath the roof of this house."

She wrapped her arms around his waist and pressed her cheek to his chest, right over his rapidly beating heart. His ribs ached, but he didn't care; the luxury of holding Josie far outweighed any discomfort from his fight with Jay.

"You lost years with your daughter," she said softly.

He couldn't miss the regret in her voice, and it made him love her all the more. "I plan to make up for lost time."

She lifted her head to look up at his face. A slight frown marred her brow. "You're not angry?" she asked, a faltering quiver in her voice.

"Oh, I'm furious," he said on a mock growl, though his underlying tone lacked any ferocity. "But not at you. I understand how hurt you were, how afraid, and you did what you had to do to take care of yourself and Kellie." He stroked his hands along her spine, soothing both her and himself with the simple gesture. "I'm furious at myself for not seeing through my brother's scheme. I'm furious at myself for being so blind to the truth and not believing in you eleven years ago. Most of all, I'm sorry that you had to spend the past eleven years alone when you and Kellie should have been with me."

"How did you know Kellie was yours?" she asked, curiosity and hesitancy mingling.

He wound a soft spiral curl around his finger and breathed deeply of the light floral scent that seemed to surround him whenever she was near. "I'd like to say that I was smart enough to figure it out for myself, but today Mac gave me a lot to think about, and then suddenly, everything made perfect sense.''

Disbelief crossed her features. ''Mac knew about Kellie?''

''He suspected she was mine because of your virtuous reputation.'' He grinned when she gave him a bewildered look. He'd have to explain Mac's ''loose woman'' theory later. ''And then I started thinking about all those rumors you always referred to and realized there was only one person I could think of who would start such damaging gossip.''

''Jay,'' she said, and he knew all the pieces of the past had finally clicked together for her, too.

He nodded. ''Yeah, my brother was behind all the rumors, and he admitted to it. We had it out, and he knows exactly where my loyalties stand. Until he can accept you as my wife and Kellie as my daughter, I don't want him to be a part of our life. I'm hoping after today's confrontation he'll rearrange his priorities to include *my* family.''

Reaching up, Josie gingerly caressed the scrape on his jaw, ran those same fingers to the cut on his lip, her touch infinitely gentle. ''You fought for me?'' she whispered.

The awe in her voice humbled him. ''Yeah, I did, but I'm about eleven years behind in defending your honor.''

That brought a smile to lips he longed to kiss. ''Nobody's *ever* done that for me.''

His chest puffed out a fraction. ''Consider it my duty as your husband. I have a wife and daughter to protect, and *nobody* will ever hurt them again.''

''Oh, Seth,'' she sighed. Gently cupping his cheek in her palm, she rose on tiptoe to show her gratitude with a kiss to the uninjured corner of his lip.

''Mom?''

Josie jumped away from Seth as Kellie's voice cut through the haze of need that had woven her in its seductive spell. She'd forgotten about her daughter, had no idea how long she'd been standing in the archway watching her and Seth or what part of their conversation she might have overheard.

Judging by the confusion shimmering in Kellie's gaze, she'd heard enough to draw her own conclusions.

Slowly, Seth turned around to face Kellie, and the two stared at one another. Kellie's eyes were huge, as if she was seeing a giant for the first time. But the adoration and love shining in Seth's eyes made Josie realize that he'd never, ever hurt her daughter.

Their daughter.

A knot formed in her chest. She had no idea how Kellie would react to the situation and prayed that she would accept the truth as well as Seth had.

"Kellie…" She forced herself to go toward her daughter, but Kellie paid her no attention.

"You're my…my dad?" Kellie asked Seth tentatively. She stood there with the first-aid supplies Josie had requested in her arms, seemingly dazed by the revelation. "My *real* dad?"

Seth glanced at Josie, silently seeking her permission to confirm the truth. Her barely perceptible nod was all he needed to say, "Yeah, I'm your dad." His voice was husky with the same emotions that brightened his eyes.

Kellie glanced at Josie, wanting to believe Seth but still needing her mother's approval. "Is he, Mom?" she asked.

That knot grew tighter, seemingly wrapping around her vocal cords. "Yes, he is." It was one of the hardest things she'd ever had to say. It was also the sweetest and most gratifying confession she'd ever made because it set a part of her free.

Kellie moved into the kitchen and set the bandages, antiseptic and cotton swabs on the table, then pinned Josie with an accusing look. "How come you never told me?"

Guilt swamped Josie, and she grappled for a feasible

answer that would explain her actions, yet make her daughter understand that her choices hadn't been easy ones. "Because...I..." An appropriate response eluded her, and she panicked, looking to Seth for help.

"The reason she never told you about my being your dad," he smoothly interjected, "was because your mother and I have been through a lot, and it was up to me to be truthful with her before she could share the truth about things with you."

Kellie was still too young to understand everything that had happened to her and Seth over the years. Though Seth's simplified explanation seemed to pacify her on some level, her worried expression told Josie that she was nervous about Seth's accepting her as his own daughter.

Seth was quick to still that particular fear because it seemed to echo his own. "I'd like the chance to make up for lost time," he said, the hope in his voice unmistakable. "I don't know much about being a dad, but I was hoping that we could learn together."

Kellie offered a pretty, accepting smile that warmed Josie's heart. "I suppose I could teach you a few things."

The tension in Seth's broad shoulders eased. "You'll find that I'm a quick learner."

Kellie shifted on her feet, her shy expression reflecting a new uncertainty. "Can I...can I call you Dad?"

Seth took a deep breath that expanded his chest. Then a huge smile creased his face. "I'd really like that. Do you think I could have a hug?"

Kellie launched herself into Seth's waiting arms. He wrapped her in a fierce hug, the expression on his face one of indescribable joy. Kellie, too, looked as though she was filled with delight.

Then Seth reached for Josie, enfolding her into the embrace and completing the circle. He gave them each a kiss on the cheek, then he smiled down at Josie, the warmth and tranquillity in his gaze matching the way she felt inside.

"I didn't realize what a lucky hand I was holding during that poker game with your father," he said, shaking his head in wonder. "I won more than the Golden M. I won the love of a good woman, and a lifetime to share with my daughter and stubborn, feisty wife."

Josie laughed, the sound lighthearted and pure.

Seth attempted to look stern. "But there's one last thing I expect from you, wife."

She lifted a brow sassily and whispered in his ear so only he could hear, "That I move back into the master bedroom?" she guessed, knowing she'd be spending that night, and every night thereafter, in their bed and in his arms.

He grinned wickedly, and with his split lip and bruised face he looked like the dangerous outlaw who thrilled and excited her. "That would be a good start, but there's something else I need to hear from you."

She knew what he was asking and didn't hesitate. "How about I love you?"

"Do you?"

"With all my heart and soul, I do love you, Seth O'Connor," she solemnly vowed. "I never stopped."

He framed her face in both hands. "And you forgive me?"

She smiled gently. "Forgiveness goes both ways."

"Then I'll meet you halfway."

"Yes, I like the sound of that," she said, and brought his mouth down to hers. The kiss was tender and full of the love and forgiveness they'd both pledged.

Most importantly, it held the promise of a new beginning.

EPILOGUE

SETH strolled into the kitchen, slipped his arms around Josie as she made pancakes for a lazy Sunday breakfast and nuzzled her neck. "Mmm, what a wonderful day for a reunion."

Josie smiled as he affectionately and possessively clasped his hands over her belly, though she found his remark a little puzzling. "Reunion?"

"Did I say reunion?" He thought for a brief second. "Yeah, I guess I did."

Exasperated, she stacked the pancakes on a plate on the counter and turned in his arms. "*What* are you talking about?" He'd been in an exceptionally good mood the past three days, acting like a kid with a surprise, and she'd yet to figure out what had prompted his lively, playful behavior.

He frowned at her, ignoring her question. "Hush, while I talk to my baby."

Bending low, he pressed his cheek to her slightly rounded tummy beneath her cotton T-shirt and leggings and murmured sweet nothings to the baby growing within. It was a morning and nightly routine Seth had insisted on. Josie listened to his silly one-sided conversation and submitted to his gentle touch and tender rubs with as much pleasure as he received from the daily practice.

From the moment she announced her pregnancy, Seth had told her he didn't want to miss a moment of this child's growth, that he wanted to be as much a part of the development process as he could possibly be. After losing that opportunity with Kellie, she understood his fierce need to bond with this baby from the start. She was only in her

177

fourth month—she estimated she'd gotten pregnant their first night together—but by the time the baby was born, he or she would know their father's gentle voice.

Unable to help herself, she touched Seth's soft hair, her heart expanding with emotions so powerful, they defied words. This man she'd been forced to marry had become her best friend. He was a wonderful, caring husband, a good, loving father to Kellie, and she knew this second child of theirs would flourish with so much love and attention.

Before her emotions could get the best of her, which they frequently did these days due to hormones, Josie rolled her eyes dramatically at her daughter as if asking, Can you believe this marshmallow of a guy talking to my tummy?

Sitting at the table, Kellie grinned at Seth's openly affectionate display. Her daughter had adjusted well to the news that Seth was her father, and with every day that passed, their father-daughter relationship only grew stronger, closer. There was a natural connection between them that even the years apart hadn't been able to sever.

Their life together over the past couple of months had settled into a comfortable routine. She and Seth still argued—she wasn't about to let him get the upper hand—but their arguments were healthy and productive. And making up afterward was delightful—Seth, rogue that he was, seduced her mercilessly, holding back what she ultimately wanted until they came to a mutually satisfactory compromise. It was a frustrating but fun way to dissolve the tension between them.

Erin visited often with Brianna and Brendan, and Josie thoroughly enjoyed the other woman's company. A few weeks ago, Josie had run into Jay at the feed store in town. After the initial awkwardness of unexpectedly meeting face-to-face, Jay had stammered out an apology that seemed to encompass every wrongdoing he'd inflicted on her through the years. Knowing that was Jay's way of asking for a second chance, she graciously accepted his expressions of regret. Next week, she and Seth planned to have Jay, Erin and their children over for their first family get-together. It was a start to mending the rift between their families.

Though life had settled into a certain tranquillity, and everything seemed as perfect as a woman could ask for, there was still one thing missing from her family. Her father. She hadn't heard from him since he'd left, worried endlessly about him and missed him terribly. Whenever she mentioned her concerns to Seth, he assured her that her father would come home. She appreciated his support and optimism, but the letter her father had written to her on his departure left her with doubts.

Finally, Seth lifted his head, ending his one-way conversation with their baby. "So, what do you think it'll be, Kellie?" he asked, a mischievous sparkle in his eyes. "A boy with my brawn and manly good looks, or another girl as beautiful as you and your mother?"

"How about twins?" Kellie suggested enthusiastically. "I'd like one of each."

Josie groaned and shook her head adamantly at her daughter's overzealous request. "How about one at a time, and we'll see if we can fill your order over the next few years."

A lopsided grin crooked the corner of Seth's mouth. "You'd give me another baby?" His voice was tender and expectant.

This baby hadn't been planned—though it had been a gift and a blessing—but she'd always wanted lots of children. "I'll give you as many as you think you can handle."

His dark brows wiggled lasciviously. "Sounds like you're gonna be barefoot and pregnant for a while, wife."

She experienced a brief flutter in the pit of her belly and wondered if it was due to the sexy gleam in her husband's eyes or her baby's first movement. Before she could con-

template that thought further, the blare of a car horn outside
interrupted the moment.

"Who could that be?" Josie wondered out loud. It was
early Sunday morning, and they weren't expecting anyone.

Seth grabbed both of her hands, suddenly looking boy-
ishly nervous. "Remember that reunion I mentioned earlier?"

She nodded. How could she forget such a cryptic comment?

"This is it." He blew out a long breath. "I hired a private investigator to look for your father, and he finally located him. I talked to Jake a few days ago, and this should
be him. I wanted it to be a surprise."

She swallowed back the emotion gathering in her throat.
"He came home?" she whispered, unable to believe the
wish she'd made by the creek a few months ago had come
true.

Seth grinned. "Only after I assured him that I was hope-
lessly in love with you and Kellie."

"Oh, Seth!" Wrapping her arms around her husband's
neck, she held him tight, tears of happiness filling her eyes.
What a precious gift he'd given her! "Thank you."

"Ah, Josie darlin'," he sighed blissfully, "I'd give you
the moon and stars if you asked for them."

The car horn sounded again, this time more insistently
and in longer intervals.

"Grandpa's really here!" Kellie scrambled from her
chair, running for the front door.

Josie and Seth followed, and by the time they'd reached
the porch, Kellie was already in her grandpa's arms, welcoming him back home with a fierce hug. An older woman
was standing beside Jake, someone Josie had never seen
before, but at the moment she couldn't think beyond the
fact that *her father was finally home*! And he looked
good—happy, healthy and handsome in his Wrangler jeans,
pearl-snap Western shirt and new snakeskin boots. Not at

all like the aimlessly drifting old man she'd envisioned he'd become.

Absolute joy filled Josie to near bursting, and she eagerly made her way to her father and embraced him with all the emotion she'd been holding back. "I didn't think I'd ever see you again!" she scolded like a worrisome mother. "And you probably wouldn't be here now if Seth hadn't hired a P.I. to search for you!"

"Nonsense," he scoffed gruffly, though his gaze was affectionate. "I planned on coming home when the time was right. When the P.I. approached me and told me who'd hired him, I knew it was the right time."

Josie shook her head. "But your letter...I thought you were gone for good, that you believed I'd never be able to forgive you for losing the Golden M in a poker game."

"Yeah, yeah, I know what I said in my letter," he said, waving a hand in the air as if to dismiss its importance. "It was all part of the plan."

His statement gave her a moment's pause. "What plan?" she demanded, the first glimmer of suspicion slithering through her.

Jake held up his hands in front of him. "Now, Josie girl, don't go getting all riled up on me. I did it for your own good."

"Did what for my own good?" She propped her hands on her hips and narrowed her gaze. "Out with it, Dad."

He scrubbed his fingers through his thick salt-and-pepper hair, his gaze flicking to Seth. "I never did like the O'Connors, especially you," he began reluctantly. "Because you were the smartest of the lot but foolish enough to believe the lies about my daughter when it was obvious how much Josie was in love with you."

Seth cringed in embarrassment, his tanned face taking on a slightly pink hue. "Guilty as charged," he admitted.

Jake gave a low humph, but there was no condemnation in his gaze. "I knew someone in the O'Connor family had to be behind the lies and rumors but could never pinpoint a source." He shifted his gaze back to Josie. "And through the years, while I watched you live a lonely existence, I wanted you to have better than living the rest of your days without a husband and family. You and Kellie deserved better than that."

Confusion puckered Josie's brow. "I still don't understand—"

"Hush, girl, I'm not done." He frowned sternly at her. "I suspected from the beginning that Seth was Kellie's father, even though you wouldn't admit to it. There was something special between the two of you once, before all the ugly gossip, and I hoped that with a little help you could find it again. Something had to bring the both of you back together and end the rift between the O'Connors and McAllisters, and the only way I could figure to do that was to give Seth what he wanted."

"You *gave* me the Golden M?" Seth nearly choked on a burst of laughter.

"All but handed it to you on a silver platter." Jake's expression was smug and extremely pleased. "I bluffed that last poker hand and deliberately lost the game to you."

Seth's mouth twisted wryly. "But not before demanding a few stipulations of your own, which included marrying Josie."

"Of course." Jake puffed out his chest in typical male arrogance. "I knew it was an offer you wouldn't pass up. And I knew my stubborn daughter wouldn't give up the Golden M to you, either."

Josie knew she should be upset with her father's interference, but found she couldn't summon the anger. What her father had done was sneaky and underhanded, but luckily, everything had worked out for the best.

"Grandpa, who's your lady friend?" Kellie asked, peering curiously at the pretty older woman who'd stood quietly next to Jake while he shared his story. She appeared to be near Jake's age, maybe a few years younger, with graying brown hair and kind blue eyes. She was simply dressed in faded jeans and a Western shirt that matched Jake's, giving the distinct impression that the two of them were a matched pair.

Beaming proudly, Jake gently clasped the woman's hand and drew her forward. She smiled adoringly at Jake, and a becoming blush shaded her smooth cheeks. "This here is Emmy Dalton, or rather, as of yesterday, Emmy Dalton McAllister, my new bride," Jake said, introducing her. "I met her while passing through a small town in Wyoming and I wasn't about to come back home without her."

Josie recognized the soft, loving expression on her father's face—it reminded her of the same look Seth often gave her. Josie was thrilled that after so many years her father had finally found someone to spend the rest of his life with.

"Welcome to the family," Josie said, and gave her a friendly, warm hug.

"Thank you. I was a widow before meeting Jake, and never had any children of my own."

"And now you're a grandma!" Kellie announced gleefully, giving the newest addition to their family a hug, too.

Emmy grinned, delight sparkling in her eyes. "At last, a grandchild to spoil!"

They all laughed, and Seth stepped forward, grasping Emmy's hand in a hospitable embrace. "It's nice to meet you, ma'am," he said in his best charming drawl. "Looks like we'll be building a new house on the Golden M for the newlyweds."

Jake scowled at his new son-in-law. "We ain't good enough to live in your house?"

Seth took no offense at Jake's umbrage. "There won't be any spare rooms for much longer. We plan to fill all the extra bedrooms with babies, the first of whom is due in the spring."

Jake's eyes widened in surprise. Then a jovial grin creased his face, and he slapped Seth on the back in masculine comradery. "Well, I'll be damned! Guess the two of you have settled into married life just fine."

An amused look passed between Josie and Seth, and he winked at her. Neither of them was about to enlighten Jake as to the more turbulent moments of their marriage. No, they'd let the sly devil believe his "plan" was a grand success from the beginning.

And as the years passed, Jake's matchmaking scheme would become as much of a legend as the actual McAllister and O'Connor feud, a lighthearted tale that would entertain many more generations to come.

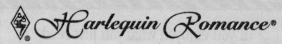
Harlequin Romance®

We're proud to announce the "birth" of a brand-new series full of babies, bachelors and happy-ever-afters: *Daddy Boom*. Meet gorgeous heroes who are about to discover that there's a first time for everything—even fatherhood!

We'll be bringing you one deliciously cute *Daddy Boom* title every other month in 1999. Books in this series are:

Who says bachelors and babies don't mix?

Available wherever Harlequin books are sold.

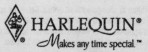
HARLEQUIN®
Makes any time special.™

Look us up on-line at: http://www.romance.net

HRDB1-R

If you enjoyed what you just read,
then we've got an offer you can't resist!

Take 2 bestselling
love stories FREE!
Plus get a FREE surprise gift!

Clip this page and mail it to Harlequin Reader Service®

IN U.S.A.
3010 Walden Ave.
P.O. Box 1867
Buffalo, N.Y. 14240-1867

IN CANADA
P.O. Box 609
Fort Erie, Ontario
L2A 5X3

YES! Please send me 2 free Harlequin Romance® novels and my free surprise gift. Then send me 4 brand-new novels every month, which I will receive months before they're available in stores. In the U.S.A., bill me at the bargain price of $2.90 plus 25¢ delivery per book and applicable sales tax, if any*. In Canada, bill me at the bargain price of $3.34 plus 25¢ delivery per book and applicable taxes**. That's the complete price and a savings of over 10% off the cover prices—what a great deal! I understand that accepting the 2 free books and gift places me under no obligation ever to buy any books. I can always return a shipment and cancel at any time. Even if I never buy another book from Harlequin, the 2 free books and gift are mine to keep forever. So why not take us up on our invitation. You'll be glad you did!

116 HEN CNEP
316 HEN CNEQ

Name	(PLEASE PRINT)	
Address	Apt.#	
City	State/Prov.	Zip/Postal Code

* Terms and prices subject to change without notice. Sales tax applicable in N.Y.
** Canadian residents will be charged applicable provincial taxes and GST.
   All orders subject to approval. Offer limited to one per household.
   ® are registered trademarks of Harlequin Enterprises Limited.

HROM99   ©1998 Harlequin Enterprises Limited

 **HARLEQUIN®**
Makes any time special™

In celebration of Harlequin®'s golden anniversary

Enter to win a *dream!* You could win:

- A luxurious trip for two to *The Renaissance Cottonwoods Resort* in Scottsdale, Arizona, or
- A bouquet of flowers once a week for a year from **FTD**, or
- A $500 shopping spree, or
- A fabulous bath & body gift basket, including **K-tel's** *Candlelight and Romance* 5-CD set.

Look for **WIN A DREAM** flash on specially marked Harlequin® titles by Penny Jordan, Dallas Schulze, Anne Stuart and Kristine Rolofson in October 1999*.

 FTD

RENAISSANCE.
COTTONWOODS RESORT
SCOTTSDALE, ARIZONA

 K·TEL

*No purchase necessary—for contest details send a self-addressed envelope to Harlequin Makes Any Time Special Contest, P.O. Box 9069, Buffalo, NY, 14269-9069 (include contest name on self-addressed envelope). Contest ends December 31, 1999. Open to U.S. and Canadian residents who are 18 or over. Void where prohibited.

PHMATS-GR

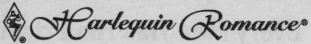

ℋarlequin Romance®

**brings you four very special weddings to
remember in our new series:**

WHITE WEDDINGS

True love is worth waiting for....

Look out for the following titles by some of
your favorite authors:

August 1999—SHOTGUN BRIDEGROOM #3564
Day Leclaire

Everyone is determined to protect Annie's good name and ensure
that bad boy Sam's seduction attempts don't end in the
bedroom—but begin with a wedding!

September 1999—A WEDDING WORTH WAITING FOR #3569
Jessica Steele

Karrie was smitten by boss Farne Maitland. But she was
determined to be a virgin bride. There was only one solution:
marry and quickly!

October 1999—MARRYING MR. RIGHT #3573
Carolyn Greene

Greg was wrongly arrested on his wedding night for something he
didn't do! Now he's about to reclaim his virgin bride when he dis-
covers Christina's intention to marry someone else....

November 1999—AN INNOCENT BRIDE #3577
Betty Neels

Katrina didn't know it yet but Simon Glenville, the wonderful doctor
who'd cared for her sick aunt, was in love with her. When the time
was right, he was going to propose....

Available wherever Harlequin books are sold.

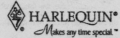

HARLEQUIN®
Makes any time special.™

HRWW

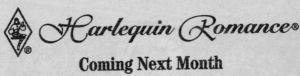

Harlequin Romance®

Coming Next Month

#3567 TRIAL ENGAGEMENT Barbara McMahon
It was Mike Black's job to keep Candee safe until she testified in court—
and his idea of protection was hiding out with her at his brother's ranch
and pretending she was his fiancée! Candee was attracted to Mike, but
he knew better than to get involved with her, however hard she was to
resist...

#3568 ONE BRIDE DELIVERED Jeanne Allan
Cheyenne's response to a newspaper advertisement looking for a
mother led her to an orphaned boy and his uncle, Thomas Steele.
Thomas clearly had no place in his life for family or for love. But
Cheyenne knew that if she could draw out the softer side to his nature
he'd make the perfect father—and husband!

Hope Valley Brides: *Four weddings and a family!*

#3569 A WEDDING WORTH WAITING FOR Jessica Steele
Karrie had been the envy of all her colleagues when they found out she
was dating company executive Farne Maitland... But Farne was a man of
the world, while Karrie's upbringing had made her determined to be a
virgin bride. There was only one solution—marry and quickly!

White Weddings: *True love is worth waiting for...*

#3570 AND MOTHER MAKES THREE Liz Fielding
When James Fitzpatrick mistook Bronte for the mother who had
abandoned his little girl, Bronte realized he must have confused her
with her career-minded sister. But James was so handsome, and his
daughter so adorable that Bronte couldn't resist slipping into the role.
What would they do when they discovered that Bronte wasn't quite who
she seemed?